Endless Endings

Neva Lukić
Endless Endings

Translated by
Jeremy White

bokeh ✳

© Neva Lukić, 2018
© Bokeh, 2018

Translated by Jeremy White
This book was published with the financial support
of the Ministry of Culture of the Republic of Croatia

Leiden, NEDERLAND
www.bokehpress.com

ISBN 978-94-91515-98-9

NON-EVENT

The beauty lay in our unspoken agreement to always succeed in not running into each other on the street. In freedom
of movement within movable borders. In the gaps in space
directed by the choreography of our bodies… Unknowingly,
we became as dynamic as a flock of birds while we marvelled
at the flocks above us. Out of our own self-directedness, our
own etched trajectories of the day, we respected the laws of
choreography that we had been subjected to. The reality, larger
than ever, lay in the very fact that we truly kept from running
into each other day after day! It lay in this non-event — one
that, again, could have happened so easily. Did daydreaming
about its nullification — about the gentle collision of bodies
on some large street somewhere in the world — solidify the
reality of its reality even further, or did this very fact transform it into an un-reality? There were no lofty goals at hand
here, only the countless possibilities of such an easily movable
motion, one that lay dormant within our bodies. Just like the
motion of a word we could so easily say to someone, but cannot,
because it catches on the tips of our tongues. We are heavy boxes
filled with endless unrealised possibilities of motion. We are
everything that did not happen today, nor will happen! That
which exists, but remains unseen by our eyes. A hidden, dark
side — a shadow of ourselves that swallows up what we were
just thinking about… Somewhere between the world of those
firmly embedded, obtrusive things that constantly force us to
move them or avoid them, and the world of birds, which casts
each movement of ours into the endless, free space above us

— there we lie, creatures of thought, creatures of shadow. We balance on the border of a kind of repressed motion, damned to walk on the surface and willingly stop, and then move, stop, move... And, out of the very fact that we are condemned to motion and freedom of immobility, this thought of ours seems to spring forth. Every day, we walk down the street and we do not run into each other. All of us, each day after we get home, can dream about tomorrow's collision of bodies on the street, about a space that breaks. About cracking. About something, it seems, so easily transpirable. It might seem to us that this is how the Sun survives — through energy created by motions that shouldn't have happened. We are free to decide, tomorrow morning when we head somewhere, that we will all collide on the street! Softly, gently... But, when the morning comes, everything will be the same again, and in the evening, we will think about the same thing. And so endlessly on and around... We are programmed like even the best of satellites, whose trajectories are, nonetheless — curved.

GRASSHOPPERS

People are no more than unusual seeds. They bring tall grasshoppers to mind. Their shapes jutting out on all sides. Limbs. Noses. And their fingers... Their faces wait, day after day. Their faces, from which — *something* — will be erased.

Sometimes it happens that I cross the street and see the world as it is, a world from which the roof of dreams has been ripped... The grasshoppers, lost, beat their wings unpredictably. Endlessly, for days on end, weaving up and down the streets. Their bodies warped, they stretch unnaturally into the heights, compressed by the sky, the Earth.

All of a sudden — hop! A handful of grasshoppers simultaneously jump to the other side of the street... Tired of their tentacles protruding out on all sides... They shut their eyes and ice up. A few of them, still moving up and down, come to help. In jerky, quick motions, they bring cement and begin filling all the empty spaces in the bodies of the frozen grasshoppers. They fill their mouths so they don't protest, they fill their nostrils, they fill their ears... They fill their vaginas so life doesn't somehow find a way out, they fill the gaps between their fingers, amputated in some other time...

After they finally fill the very last empty space, they receive the order to perfect every form. They take more cement and turn the petrified grasshoppers into triangles, squares, spheres, and trapezoids... In order to give the impression that the world is multifarious...

Around me now, squares, rolling spheres, and shadows. In their own dry spaces where it never rains. An ambulatory grasshopper or two pass by who will perhaps keep on going endlessly, up and down, ever a seed...

All of a sudden — hop! One of the shapes suddenly flinches to the other side of the street. For a time, it simply stands there, frozen... Noiselessly, as if it isn't there, a drop slides down his plane, leaving the moment unscathed. Water created within comes to the surface, finding space through the walls. A cramped, empty place... The way.

Beneath his eyelids, the face of a grasshopper looms... He opens his eyes and lets the space around him inside him.

Water keeps rolling down his face. As if nothing is happening, invisibly, it creates a story. A cramped empty place. A slot that holds the world.

The face of man waits patiently, his face from which — *something* — will arise.

Pandora's Box

In the beginning, the mouth was closed, a soft roundness like the Earth; inside, words glowed like fireflies and sung like cicadas. The orifice opened for no one, nor did it say anything — words reflected within it like smooth stones in the crystalline, rippling water of a cave. There were more words inside than there are bacteria on a fingertip. They would float in the airless space, until the lazy Tongue would wake from his sleep and touch them with his slumberous, warm body to give them form, if only for a moment. The cave would then flash as bright as day — sometimes from the light of just one word, which would soon extinguish like a torch, and sometimes from an entire choir of sentences. The words were satisfied with this. They were only occasionally bothered by the fact that there was no space between the teeth, which made it impossible for them imagine they were walking through the streets — all they could do was jump along a toothed wall. Otherwise, life was exactly as it should have been... Periods of time passed in which the words existed from within — calm and embodied, they created combinations no one could either see or hear. They became real only for some higher being, as if they were priests in the holiest part of the temple... But soon, an unimaginable restlessness took hold of the Tongue. He could no longer bear the fact that he had been harnessed like some dangerous beast since the moment of his creation! Born in chains. He had never been free. His long, insufficiently ramified form did not allow him to make contact with himself — he could only touch the teeth or the flesh of the cheek, and neither of these things made any

difference to him in his life whatsoever. He asked himself —
what was his purpose in this world? He could not even perceive
himself, let alone walk freely about the mouth, as the words
could. Why, was he only here because of them? Only to caress
them? Who would caress him?! The Tongue began to thrash
about the mouth, harnessed and tied like a sorrowful, freshly
awakened volcano. He strained against all sides of the mouth
like a reined horse, but he was so soft that he hurt no one; he
was so silent that no one heard him. A limp, slimy beast. He
couldn't even scatter the teeth about the mouth and turn them
into a small town, to give the words the gift of streets! He
realized that he was an unnecessary anomaly of the world. This
drove him mad — so much so that, one day, he became so
angry that he tripled in mass. Out of helplessness, he began to
toss himself around the orifice like a great bludgeon. Finally
— and entirely by accident (as the Tongue hadn't dreamt that
some world outside his own might exist) — he poked a small
hole in the roundness, and it let in a pale light similar to what
the words would give off when he brushed against them. He
got the urge to dash out of his claustrophobic pit, but even if
the opening hadn't closed soon afterwards, it wouldn't have
been possible, because he was sewn into the tissue with threads
stronger than the firmest steel chains. All he could do was rear
up on his atrophied hind legs and growl angrily like a guard
dog. If he had a knife — or if he even had hands at all — he
could have taken that knife and at least raised his hand against
himself and cut through the root that made him into the most
ordinary, dullest of trees. He could go nowhere. He had to
stand in this small place until he died. A Prometheus in chains,
pecking at his own liver day after day in the moist, dark hole
of his own Hades. He sighed, happy for a moment as the hole
had closed, and hope along with it… Full of strength, muscu-
lar, mobile in every direction and yet accursedly immobile, his

body began to heave with dry tears, while the words inside remained full, as if underwater. Compressed like soft tissue, like a gentle balloon, they embodied the entire roundness, which changed form in accordance with their phases. Its form could never be repeated exactly. Within their phases, the words were as purposeful as bees, each with their own structure and function. They gathered honey in the mouth. They created it together... But alas, the poor Tongue couldn't leave well enough alone, and he finally thought of something — if he himself couldn't leave, he would launch the words out through the opening like a catapult, and they would tell him what was outside! They would be his slaves — he would make them go out, in, out, in at his whim. The words would live between two worlds. As if someone were to push their heads underwater every once in a while and then give them a little air again, and then push their heads under, and then give them a little air... That is how their life would be. What could he do — even that was certainly better than his life... They were at least free inside and would be free outside, so they had to help him a bit, his only compatriots. The Tongue grabbed hold of a few of them firmly, pinning them against his tip, and then he blew them towards the opening. He waited tensely for a few moments to see what would happen, and sure enough, luck was on his side — the opening swallowed the words, and the Tongue was again left in darkness. He began to flail about the orifice for joy! He had done it! All he had to do was call them back in, and they would once again appear there, his secretaries, his slave girls. He took another hundred-odd words and launched them all out. The opening obediently swallowed them, constantly opening, closing, until not a single word was left inside. The Tongue proudly strolled about his chamber, convinced that a kingly cape had grown around his body. He decided to doze a while, and then call his flock home. When he awoke, he spoke their names, and the entire army appeared beside him in an instant, coming in just as they had gone out. The Tongue began to chuckle smugly, and his laugh hid a hint of spite. He ordered them to inform him immediately about everything they had seen, and they resignedly began to speak of the soft lips, through whose circulation and warmth they had slipped into a world full of human beings and wars... Finally, the words had discovered what they meant — before, they had only created their own personal meanings, which had no connection to the meaning the external world had given them... Used to his and their old tongue, the Tongue suddenly realized that he understood nothing they were saying to him. The new language these madwomen were speaking had no meaning to him. Out of anger, he spit them out again! And so it went day after day; he would spit them out, not thinking about what he was saying. Speech had no meaning to him. He would simply throw the words out, over and over again. The more of the world they saw, the further from him they grew and the less he understood them. They also began to feel meaningless, torn between worlds, lost in dimensions. Unity and harmony no longer existed. The words were wasted over and over again, the Tongue consumed them without understanding, punishing them for avoiding him, as now they could leave on their own! He hated both them and himself. He constantly sent them out so he wouldn't have to look at them. Besides, they were speaking completely different languages by now. He didn't understand a single, solitary word spoken in his own kingdom of words. He knew they were hooking up with all manner of new sentences and types of words out there, and they knew they were unsatisfied, but still, they had to go out. Pandora's box had been opened. There was no going back. The Tongue felt as if he were in an even greater hell than before. He was no longer even angry — only resigned. Little by little, he began to notice that the opening was growing larger and larger, as the words would wear it down a bit every time they passed through it. The mouth's blabbering stretched it out more and more, and soon it took up the entire curved surface. A gaping emptiness had come into the world. The Tongue had finally managed to free himself and hide like a mute worm in some crack in the earth. The words scattered about the world, and not a single one was left for him. Today, this mute worm can be found in stony caves on certain islands. Some scientists claim that this creature feeds on insects and, like sea creatures, is aware of nothing. Others, however, expound an entirely different theory. They say the being captures tourists' words with the tip of its flat, long body. Then it drags them into the cave, where it caresses them and pours water over them so that they might stay forever, so they might never evaporate, at least not so long as he exists on the Earth.

The Universe

I believe I am in the place where it all might have begun. And it didn't begin at all like we thought it did… It's entirely different than we thought, and yet entirely simple, inverted. This contradiction wasn't easy to comprehend, but perhaps that was the very thing we misinterpreted to begin with…

I find myself in a world in which pictures have become immaterial like words, and words have become a tangible material, pure pigment. And music — music dwells in the willowy frames of mute flocks of white birds that fly over the water and then suddenly disappear, each sliding into the distance in its own key… Here I am, I walk this space in which matter has become equal to the boundedness of words, and such places are as rare as solar eclipses. It's rare that everything falls into place and stays that way. I feel as if I'm walking through the abandoned cities of a failed civilisation, walking through Cusco, which the Sisyphean Europeans first destroyed and buried just so they could find it again a few hundred years later; as if the streets are empty, but aren't. Something is unusual in this place, everything seems to be something else, the inverse of itself… The place is full of people, and yet it seems empty; here, words become architecture, and architecture becomes intangible like words… Why? Has the eclipse frozen over?

It seems as if the word "house" and an actual "house" live in balance here. "House" and "House" have merged into one, into an eclipse. Are they not — as people are when they connect — nothing more than an eclipse, a perfect circular darkness with light pouring out from behind it? Here, "House" and "House" exist in harmony, without the discrepancy that is so common in their relationship. The reflections of houses don't radiate too many colours, so that they don't rise above the word like a bird and make it small, small, helpless... The very word, however, portrays only a picture, like a silent film. It's reticent enough not to rise up, crowing, above a "building that has walls and a roof and serves for human habitation..." So, allow me to build you the place where I find myself:

House House House House House House
House House House House House House
House House House House House House
House House House House House House

Just like this. Not a gram more. Here, the words "House" and "A building that has walls and blah blah blah..." are in perfect balance on the seesaw. This is a special state. Like when a dowsing rod begins to tremble above an underground spring...

And the people who walk the "pavement" (*lat.* pavire: beat, tread down), which beats like a drum (when it is full of voices), which is downtrodden (when it is silent and introverted), are the true humanity. Again, the word "humanity" and "the human race, the sum total of all people" are in an absolute balance on the scales. The word "humanity" is jammed between house and house and house and house... Vivid, it stretches across the grey streets like laundry hung out on a line.

House	H	House
House	u	House
House	m	House
House	a	House
House	n	House
House	i	House
House	t	House
House	y	House

The world around me is basic — it is the basic structure language offers me when I say: "Humanity is here among these houses."

The foundation of language manifests itself in physical form, offering me its basic skeleton, and around it I build pictures, which are exclusively intangible here.

I see the Tower of Babylon, which might have stood here once. A spiral ziggurat that never managed to reach the heavens, because its steps grew ever narrower, narrower, narrower, while human feet grew larger from step to step... Or did the ziggurat reach the heavens unpeopled and keep travelling, unable to find a particle that cannot be split, that cannot be made into a new particle-step? I see it, I see the Tower of Babylon still travelling, as it will for eternity...

I find myself in a place inhabited by humanity, in a city that speaks hundreds of languages — a city that, viewed as a whole, has actually attained God. The walls of its "Houses" understand the melodies of the various languages spoken within them. Melodies of languages, like the melodies of the "white birds" that fly above everything and everyone, the only ones irreducible to the skeleton of language, the frame around which meat grows... "Birds" is not a sufficient word to describe the white birds. It's as if they fell out of this city and became embodied in the sky, where they live their lives in some other dimension. They fell out of the system, one that was perhaps invented for the members of humanity who walk these pavements and don't understand each other. The city might have reached outer space through these languages, but unfortunately, the individuals it is composed of can't function as a whole if they continue speaking their native tongues. This is why language is reduced to its base here, to a visual form, a construction. So that foreigners are somehow able to communicate...

And at that moment, I realise that people did not create languages — languages created people. At that moment, I realise that I am at the very centre, the "holy of holies," a temple of around six thousand gods (linguists don't know how many there are exactly)!

Once, long ago, languages only lived within sounds. At the very beginning, they weren't yet bothered by this — still unpolished, each of them was still being created out of its own essential sound. Some arose from the sloshing of the sea in hollow spaces (French), some from a punishing westerly wind that won't let up, some from the drumming of the rain, some from the clip-clop of hooves (Macedonian), some from the sliding of snow off of mountaintops (British English comes to mind)… But one is still being created out of the melody of birds in flight, and that's why — why, that's why those birds fly free and embodied in this world! Above humanity, a language is being born! As the years passed, the languages continued to polish themselves, becoming more and more complete — true, mature gentlemen. When they finally came of age, they naturally got the urge to have an intelligible conversation with someone! Language couldn't talk to itself, because it was too caught up in itself to be able to hear itself. This is how it was for every language — every language felt like the next language and every other language, and the languages were never more united than when they couldn't communicate. Little by little, like some strange fruit, they began to ooze those for whom no word yet existed. Many unusual, new beings appeared, "the most highly developed beings on Earth", who called themselves "people". No one asked the languages anything anymore. But they were happy, because they could finally communicate amongst themselves, in a way at least: through glances, touches, and pictures. This is enough for them. This sound of silence.

And here I am in their temple. In the temple of universality. In the universe.

Skysilk[1]

Atop thick walls near the clouds, in a high, roofless building, there lived a man. He couldn't see the bottom of his building with the naked eye; off in the distance, like the lights of a far city, he could only make out its furniture. The little dots that buzzed around the furniture might have been some kind of living beings, beings similar to him, but he couldn't be sure of that. There had never been anyone around him… Had he just woken from a dream, or had he just been born? He couldn't know… But the time of anticipation began to flow… With each passing hour, the weight in his stomach grew in step with his thoughts… As if by miracle, even though he had no mother, he knew how to shape his thoughts in his mother tongue, and he felt a great urge to place his complaints on someone else's lips… He tried with the birds, but they only squawked from the nests they had built on the building's rim, and their noises only silenced him further… Every once in a while, he would stuff his mouth with a stolen egg, fearing their sharp beaks. In times of despair, he would even try to convince himself he was one of them, for what other role was there for him to play in this story? He would then touch his soft nose with his fingers, or he would try to spread his arms into wings, and all hope would evaporate in an instant. He would shrug his shoulders and longingly observe those free creatures as they formed a flock

---

[1]   The original title of this story in Croatian, *Čovječina*, is a play on the word *paučina* (spider web), in which 'spider' (*pauk*) is replaced with 'man' (*čovjek*). A literal translation of the original title would be "human web" or "human silk".

in the air, a latticework dome atop the sky. He would also stuff the occasional wandering insect into his mouth, swallowing it in confusion. His landscape consisted of the tops of the clouds, and his best friends were the birds, whose embrace he had never felt! They nested, and he slept on his feet, like a real live bird! He instinctively longed for countless steps — should this not have been his innate manner of expression? This is what his thoughts whispered to him, at any rate.

Inspired by a mixture of unbearable feelings, he began to feel himself out. He kissed his hands, feet, fingers, whispering his ails to them with his touch. He was sure, as he was the only human in his surroundings, that the "true him" was located in the only place his eye could not see, and that was his head. It was the only thing he experienced as his very own, while everything that surrounded it, everything he could see, seemed to possess its own individuality. Kissing his hand, he felt as if he were kissing someone else. He would even occasionally talk with it, forgetting about the chirping of the birds. At his words, the fingers merely sighed, until one day, firm, transparent strands of saliva begun to hang from them. As hard as crystal, as long as entrails, as flexible as fingers. This was the moment in which the man began to build a structure he knew from somewhere as "spider silk" — instead, he called it "skysilk". He certainly didn't consider himself a spider. If there was one thing he believed, it was that he wasn't an arthropod.

Frightened, he stood at the edge of the city cliff, his bulging eyes staring into space, as if he had just witnessed some evil, paranormal creature. He stood arched above the nothingness, imagining his first steps. The abyss was more frightening than anything else, and it made his heart pound fastest. The love-induced pounding of the heart is child's play in comparison to this shot of adrenaline… He kissed his hands firmly, as if this were the last time he would see them, and the first, long line of silk stuck to the wall of the building opposite, continuing out of the life line on his palm. He knew he had to walk across the strand to continue to build. When he looked at the barely visible line, which seemed to be made of nothing more than air in some different state of aggregation, his face sobered. Tightrope walkers first walk on the earth, but he would take his first steps under the sky. Tightrope walkers can lose their lives, but he could only gain a life. He wasn't a tightrope walker. The man bravely outstretched his leg, spreading his arms like wings. After two steps, the strand began to sway, and he was left on all fours in the air. Thankfully, the strand was slippery, and so he managed to stretch himself prone and slide across it to the other side in just a few moments. Sweaty, he abandoned his unstable position and sat on the wall. He had only managed to crawl quickly across instead of walking, but it was a good start. He decided to cross the rest of the strands in the same way. Full of joie de vivre, this time, he passionately kissed his golden hand. The juices remained in his mouth for some time. With all his strength, he stretched another tight strand across the air — it glinted like a long raindrop, vanishing into a squat tunnel of clouds in the distance. He stepped out even more bravely than the first time — and why not? His strands were only a variation on the theme of the floor! If people believed in the concrete someone else had put beneath their feet (his thoughts also whispered him this fact), why shouldn't he believe in his very own silk, which was sensitive to his touch, and not to tremors imposed by outside forces? He resolutely decided to take a walk through his new, taut habitat. Calm and collected, he succeeded in taking a few steps, as if he were walking a land yet untouched. The shapes beneath him were too far away for him to see. He felt like a huge bird of prey with its wings outstretched over all of existence. He ruled, because he was now lighter than the strands, his very being making him most akin to a cloud. After about four steps, a sudden fear took hold of him for a moment, and the strand began to sway from left to right. In the end he crawled across again, this time hanging beneath the strand. He dozed on the thick, sun-warmed walls, a deep belief in the future within him.

In the coming days, he repeated the process, and soon the lines had turned into a web that was still oversaturated with gaps. He began to add onto it in the crawling position, which he soon mastered. It grew diligently day by day out of the loneliness of kisses... Regular threads grew out of the centre of the skysilk in a unidirectional spiral, making the web reminiscent of the round webs woven by some species of spider. The man had managed it unintentionally, but how he had was unclear to him. The other side was criss-crossed with a web of diverse strands that formed no shape whatsoever. Literally, not metaphorically, they represented the paths of his life, continuing out of the life, heart, head, health, and fate lines on his palms. This was a man who had nothing else... In his case, symbolism had become reality, while reality was symbolically unfolding somewhere else... Amidst that jumble of threads, at least he could finally find respite from birds and kisses in his unusual love nest! If palmistry were to be believed, he would live at least five hundred years, so he was in no hurry... Of course, he still crawled clumsily around the skysilk, feeling its threads encompass him sensually. Unsure of their firmness, he clung to them meekly, not knowing if he were more afraid for his own life or for the life of the web. He didn't yet dare give himself over to the unknown work woven of his own fingers. With veneration, he observed its beauty, simultaneously flat and round, strong and fragile. It was something new and fascinating, a meaning for his life that was finally tactile. You could say, word for word: "It was the very ground he stood on!" He groped along uncertain paths, not daring to put his weight on his own feet. It seemed as if his steps would destroy it, and that the gaps in it would lead him to his downfall. He also feared storms, certain that the squalls and winds would lay waste to it. He awaited the first wind with bated breath... But when it finally came, nothing bad happened. The skysilk only undulated and held him even more tightly! He happily informed his hand that everything had ended well, after all.

Days passed, the birds squawked, and the man moved more and more confidently about the skysilk with each passing moment. Each morning, whistling in chorus with the birds (their chirping now pleased him), he would fill the emptiness of the air with at least one more life line. As if it were he, and not the painter Appel, who had said "Nulla dies sine linea." He became a more and more skilful builder, crawling through his construction with gusto.

He realised that there was little chance it would be destroyed, and so he could finally stretch out in his bed and relax like a human being! He said goodbye to the standing bird within him. His bed did have holes in it, however, and his limbs constantly fell out into the ether... But he tried to enjoy the lightness of this existence, because he was far more comfortable than ever before... He didn't want to practice sleeping on the strands — that would mean sleeping tense, allowing his own bed to rule him! No, no, no. It was better he sent his limbs out to play. Because, as we have already mentioned, he didn't perceive them as a part of him, not only because he greatly noticed how different they were from him, but because they constantly distanced themselves from him. Regardless, he still nested clumsily amidst the lines of his life.

The man finally made his home in the skysilk, and life became easier.

The skysilk also became multifunctional. All manner of animals, already baked and sliced, began to fall into the web of his life. He had never seen these animals before, and unfortunately he couldn't know what they had looked like while they were still breathing, as they didn't look all that different from each other when they were baked. He only noticed the difference in taste between chicken, pork, venison, veal, beef... Fish would sometimes get caught in the web, and then he was happy, because only they were in one piece and looked similar dead as they had alive. Their meat was the blandest, but the days with fish were his best days. Sitting on the airy tiles of his kitchen, he would gobble them down hungrily. He could barely wait to reach the heart of the nearness of bones and separate them from the meat. He especially loved fish bones — they reminded him of a fossilised feather, or fossilised flight. Of love, of freedom, of his skysilk... After eating, or at any other time, a shower from the sky would sometimes mercifully wash him in the deep tub in his bathroom, allowing him to return to the abandon of his dreams unsoiled.

The man ceased perceiving the exceptional flexibility of his web. He got used to its wind-shaped form. With time, when he finally perfected his monkey-spider skills, he would begin every morning by kissing his hands in a frenzy so that he might weave as many strands as possible. The saying grew heavier — "Nulla dies sine *quinquae* lineae!" He was tired of constantly crawling. He wanted to be able to lie, walk, stand, sit. A skeleton of a house was no longer enough for him, and he longed to fill in the gaps. As he possessed no bricks, he focused on the only building material available to him.

Life flowed from day to day, becoming firmer with each new morning. The feathery skysilk soon turned into what he knew as a cocoon — he renamed it a 'skycoon'. Its roof grew, encircling him entirely, just like the curve of the earth surrounds the insects in the planet's womb. It became so firm that it no longer seemed as if the stitches would break, requiring him to patch them with tired kisses. It became as thick as carpet, and there was less and less air within it. He finally managed to stand on his own two feet, and with great effort, he could even sit! As he changed positions, he enjoyed his own corporeality. But the sky-coon pressed in on him ever more closely, and soon his solitary limbs were bound up against him. He was like a "tightly-knit personality" within his own larva! In such a state, he dreamt of gaps, those gaps he once had more of than he knew what to do with. If only he had just one hole through which to throw himself into life!

This was when the man realised that intangibility is much more fragile than tangibility.

Of course, he blamed the damned skysilk for having woven the web around him! But it was too late for thinking, now that he could finally hold fast to the walls of his three-dimensional skycoon.

He remained standing.

He never fell.

The man truly never experienced a (down)fall.

He really did "fulfil" his greatest wish: he became embodied forever. The birds above his head chirped the life eternal.

LINES

Know the world is a mirror from head to foot,
In every atom are a hundred blazing suns.
If you cleave the heart of one drop of water,
A hundred pure oceans emerge from it.

Mahmud Shabistari, Gulshan-i-rāz

I have a friend who is obsessed with lines. Everything of his — the old tightrope walker — always has to be in line so he doesn't accidentally cross any borders. We haven't seen each other for years because of this, we always talk over a telephone line! At least then we're in line with each other, he says, but I truly don't understand. I think he may have begun to put too much faith in modern channels of communication...

But he says we would be separate individuals if we saw each other in real life, and he's had enough of outlines and borders. This way, we are one, our voices travel together through the telephonic ether: HELLO? HELLO? HELLO?!

I think some of his curves have become a bit bent. I've tried to explain to him countless times that face-to-face communication is much better... But he won't budge, he says that we're a part of the random chaos of the world in real life, that we're each scattered on our own lines, on parallel courses, in parallel universes.

And so I've been hearing about lines for years now, sitting with him for hours on the telephone line. I've already told him I'm not sure it's really all because of lines, or perhaps that's just the line of least resistance! No, no, no — he stubbornly claims that the lines of footsteps are sloppy and irregular, and that they never meld into one. Everything should be a part of the same ball of yarn! He seethes... The world mustn't be rent apart by that damned division between animate and inanimate lines. He also relates his own mortality to yarn, believing he'll live longer if he doesn't throw himself around along various lines, like Tarzan. Instead, he lives a life that is — like the life of a ball of yarn — one single line.

He always tells me, you'll see, my dear, I'll live to at least two hundred, because it's a hard and uncommon thing to live on the line, to always be on the edge. There's a lot you have to give up on...

Right... According to what I've managed to gather from our multi-minute conversations:

"Animate lines", Mother Lines, thin shells of enthusiasm that hang elastically in gaps, creating meat and breath. They don't get tangled up in the outside world, although they are deeply entangled in it. Within everything, they are outside everything in everything. They only lead an internal life by silently transferring material and signals to various places. They are the "No-Man's Land" after which everything is modelled — they, the mothers of outlines. They stretch freely through air, meat, water, describing nothing.

"Inanimate lines" are their expression, their frozen tentacles embroidering space, describing various kinds of animate and inanimate things to fill the gaps of their hungry mothers. They always close off or limit things, convincing life of its own diversity, convincing the world of the existence of the world and reality!

At this point, he touches again on his desire for all of us to be connected through knots on the same line, which will then prove that all forms of "inanimate lines" around us are nothing more than a fabrication that arose from the ability of separateness — or rather parallelism — to exist.

Those bloody inanimate lines, he fumes, we just need to get rid of them somehow and the truth will come out! The parallel lines will finally interpermeate completely, and the apparent possibility of metaphor will disappear...

Hmmm, I'm not sure. The disappearance of metaphor, really? What sort of stylistic trick *is* that? I warn him...

But he claims this is the only path to unity... Metaphor must disappear in style so that my friend can prove what metaphor already proved so long ago. But, of course, no one ever gave a hoot about (the intangibility of) words.

And then, one day, about two weeks ago, after years and years of conversations, a telephone call woke me at three in the morning. On the other end of the line, a euphoric voice asked if I could feel something unusual in the air! I don't know, I don't think so, I said drowsily, sniffing at the space around me, but he continued as if he hadn't heard... After hours and hours of studying comparability, he had finally come close to finding tangible evidence! He realised that when "animate lines" of the same species mix, they then create "inanimate lines", forms that lead to separation, to an endless number of various universes that are actually false! In the world we have known until now, "animate lines of the same species" have always been connected, without exception. That was the rule! Then they would take on various forms and outlines, and so metaphor in that world had room for "as" and "like"... He had to share this discovery with me while there was still time! He, he had decided to deviate from the rule and connect "different kinds of animate lines of different strains", and not just the same kind like he had before — not just those that created edges together! People, Plants, Buildings! Automobiles, Computers, and Animals! Do you understand?!

His lines flow, his paths lead only to paths... Electric cables to veins and capillaries, neurons to water pipes...

Unbelievable, he can't believe his eyes! And yet he can never show his discovery to anyone, because it would mean his "lines are crossed"!

See, the monster is about to start breathing, he yells breathlessly into the receiver. A brittle monster on the floor of his subterranean flat... A living metaphor! A metaphor at a lower level! "Subaphor", that's what he calls it, hahaha! The closer it comes to breathing, the fewer words he feels within him. And that doesn't worry him in the least...

What a complete maniac! He called me without a second thought at three in the morning, almost certainly rubbing his palms together with glee on the other end of the line.

And to all this, of course, I reply: Hello?!

But he doesn't pay any mind; he continues on unbothered.

He says that soon, any moment now, on the floor of his room, parallel universes will cross completely and create a new universe in which parallel actions will no longer exist as a result. This could even cause time to stop, although he isn't entirely sure. We'll only find out when that new universe in his room outgrows both me and him and the cities and mountains...

Circular Paths

One day, the people of the country came to decide that they were bothered by the fact that not all people were the same height. This was perhaps the only thing they hadn't succeeded in fixing, as they simply hadn't noticed it until now. Somehow, it had more or less always been hanging above them, and not right in front of their noses! Devious, like a cancer, it had lived in their lives until the day someone realised that the state of things was abnormal — that the entire country was base and amoral because, for as long as it had existed, certain individuals had allowed themselves too much. Allowed themselves to come closer to the heavens than others. Why, it was simply an unscrupulous, discriminatory breach of human rights! In no other area was the situation as worrisome, and just when they had thought they were in control! Everything else functioned as it should — all the tram cars were the same height, all the glasses in the kitchen cupboards, all the cows in the fields, all the buildings on the lawns. Even the land itself on which all this was located was exactly as it should be — a plain adorned with only ploughed fields, lain bare of all the irregularities, curves and valleys, mountains and dunes that all other supposedly beautiful, natural countries were so full of. They were never jealous of those "beautiful" countries, because order was beauty to them. They had lived satisfied lives until the moment they realised that their bodies were so perfidiously conspiring against the state! Irreproachably, they grew beyond the designs of their borders, lines in the air within which they had only now realised they were allowed to grow! As they had never before noticed this disorderly, irregular curve, the terrifying fact that people's heights ranged in a broad spectrum from 1.50 to 2.10 metres, and that this group of numbers was innumerable! Half a metre is a significant difference in a human framework, and human frameworks require particular frameworks. The people of this country began to applaud, proud to be the first in the world to attain complete advancement, to raise themselves to the level of supermen by bringing themselves all to the same level! Civilised beings cannot grow as they please! Why, that's simply primitive, and it promotes sexual discrimination! We cannot truly say that women are emancipated while they are shorter than men, or that the races are equal in this state, in which so many nations and races live. They found this new discovery so revolutionary that it undermined all their old beliefs, and they realised that they had been living a lie and had to begin again. In the worst case, it wouldn't even be a sin to trim those who had grown too far into the sky — they would do anything at all to set things right! People can't simply grow however they like, as if they were trees! Trees are allowed to grow for specific reasons, and that wouldn't change. Trees are so disorderly in and of themselves that it makes no sense to even try dealing with them. The people of this country had given up on trees long ago, and would have thrown them out if their lives didn't depend on them. At a referendum held quite some time ago, the trees managed to scrape by, while the situation with the roses, for example, was entirely different... They long grew freely, bushes of different sizes, red as if dug out from the depths of the body, until one day they were reported to the police by Mr. G, whose balcony overlooked this wildness. Not half an hour had passed before the city services chopped them to bits. Car tyres drove mercilessly across the asphalt, covered in petals... But Mr. G's brain was still harrowed by the shrunken, flowery jungle, as its thorns still threatened the cats that skulked through it. He remembered the flowers, simultaneously open and closed, the labyrinth of petals in which Ariadne wove her web… His imagination was fired to its fullest, and soon — the good Samaritan he was — he decided to suggest a solution to the greatest problem in the country… People were worried, as if during the worst possible economic crisis or state of war. On the streets, one could often see two people talking in a special way. One of them would continuously look down, hunched over, while the other would stretch their neck out towards the heavens! How they succeeded to converse in such a state and whether their gazes ever even met was anyone's guess… These acts were probably the final nail in the coffin of communication in the state, even as its residents were convinced they were all striving towards a happy medium. Soon, everything ceased functioning as it should have; an ever-greater chaos of disharmony reigned amongst everyone. The air was thick with anxiety and animosity. On the one hand, people awaited the government's decision with apprehension — what if their decision involved interventions into the state of their bodies? On the other hand, they could not bear the disorderly line that connected all of their heads! Each new day found their patience wearing thinner, but unfortunately, solving such a problem would require many hours of work. Weakened so, what could they and their country do against the cruel fate that had beset them? What could the minuscule human race undertake against the powerful force of growth? They couldn't simply say "Stop," or "Continue." Their government surely would not follow the example of the Nazis, controlling each individual separately. First of all, this was financially impossible, and second, their state was a champion of human rights and equality! Amidst such ponderings, they were met with their government's decision, which called upon all citizens to participate in finding a solution in the true spirit of democracy. The invitation included the condition that, in the future, all citizens both male and female must be exactly one hundred seventy five centimetres tall at their twenty-fifth year of age. Around ten thousand applications were sent in, including one from Mr. G. The majority of applications were in accordance with the times in which these citizens lived: the ordinary citizenry offered cheap solutions such as chopping off heads and limbs, things they had seen in films on television, while the doctors and biologists offered expensive solutions including the administration of growth hormones or DNA editing. The engineers, however, were practical — they didn't want to change any part of the human body whatsoever. Instead, the feet of people shorter than one hundred and seventy five centimetres would be attached to a small, motorised platform that would bring their growth to the desired height, while the feet of those taller than one hundred and seventy five centimetres would be attached to the same manner of device, which would be located beneath the ground. These people would automatically become shorter, and the device would make it easier for them to walk through the earth. The review board didn't like a single one of the solutions offered. They were all either bloody or very expensive quick fixes that had nothing of a deeper nature within them. Nowhere could one feel any trace of an ideology that might represent the true reasons why the government had decided to take such extreme measures: reasons of equality, human rights, and the harmony of the golden ratio. Most solutions looked only into the future, except for that of the engineers, and even their idea did not bring any permanent, evolutionary change to their species. The remaining experts had not dealt too much with the older generations that had already grown up, instead looking at them — and thus at themselves — as the dregs of time that would only serve to help their children become perfect. Of all of the applications sent in, only one caught the commission's eye. It was Mr. G's simple suggestion, and they thought it might be able to lead them in the right direction. It contained no complicated drafts for the construction of machines, nor did it feature any high budgets for the production of miraculous hormones. There wasn't a single drop of blood in it, and Mr. G was neither a scientist nor an empty-headed member of the masses. To successfully carry out his plan, all that was needed was years of effort and millions of wooden boards — all in all, a primordial, cheap solution that was in line with the unwritten ideology of the country. Mr. G had taken everyone into account — people who were yet to grow up and those who were already grown… However, he had had to lower the limit of human height in the country to one hundred and fifty five centimetres to do so. Something had to be sacrificed, after all. Mr. G. offered the following solution. People who were not yet grown would start wearing a firm wooden frame around them during puberty — fixed at one hundred and fifty five centimetres — which would be impossible for their bodies to grow out of. Those who would remain below the limit of one hundred and fifty five centimetres would be considered exceptions in the country (as they had been until then), and the exception, as we know, proves the rule. Those generations who had long grown out of puberty would take the opposite tactic. As the goal was not to artificially intervene into their bodies, all the people in these generations would at first try to move about like slugs for at least an hour a day — to humbly slide along the earth, all more or less the same height, nearly incorporated into the flat plane of a chessboard. Depending on the results and their own achievements, they would eventually begin spending more and more time in that position. But it was the explanation included in Mr. G's solution that actually won the commission over. It was quite clear and to the point: *This solution does not contain any artificial interventions. It is only mildly aggressive and encourages a new, natural evolution of our species. It does not offer an instant solution — instead, the citizens of our state must live their lives in accordance with the philosophy written here. How is it that we, the esteemed citizens of this country, have not realised the essence of everything, the spice without which nothing truly functions, the final step we must take to make ourselves perfect and complete — to frame ourselves — until this very day?! I resorted to the simplest method — placing man within a wooden frame. This act might also evoke the suffering of our predecessor, the esteemed Jesus Christ, who bore a cross instead of a frame. Our new generations of citizens shall then also pass through a painful catharsis. On the other hand, we whose bones have already ossified shall turn submissively towards the earth like slugs, and see what sort of evolutionary path this act leads us along… Will our bones soften like rose petals? Softened like this, what course shall we take? Only time will tell…*

After ten-odd days of discussions, the review board introduced a test period for Mr. G's theory, which was to be put into effect to see how it functioned. They decided to give it a few years' time. In just a few months time, all of the larger factories were already producing wooden frames with openings for limbs, one hundred and fifty five centimetres high, suited to the human bodies of the future. The openings on the frame were fitted with soft fabric so the young ones wouldn't get blisters. Human feet and parts of the hands, in a way, became the only free parts of the body! Only the fingers lived their own lives, while everything else was shut within the frame — even young, still naïve human faces. It was necessary to enclose the entire human body inside for the scalp and shoulders to prevent it from growing and striving for the sky. They could only strive downward, where, as the older and more experienced have warned us, we will all end up. All should aspire to be the same "lowness," and to stand firmly on the ground. Yes, the people of that country no longer spoke of tallness, but "lowness". The new term fit better into the overall identity of their country, in which there were no mountains. Here, finally, everyone had to be equally short, equally small, equally submissive.

Soon, on the streets, more and more young people could be seen walking in their frames, reminiscent of living pictures, living framed art. They wore their frames proudly, as their parents had told them it would lead them to a better life. When they reached their goal, it would all result in one large, communal frame of life in and of itself, one that would no longer have to be visible to be felt. Just that one last thing, human height... Let them pay no mind to older generations, whose heads jut out incorrigibly towards the sky. Parents thus urged their descendants to make an effort to wear the frames as often as possible. They only allowed them to sleep without them, all to make the frames a component part of the bodies of their children, and thus a part of their lives. After a few years, success was apparent. Children walked the city framed but light, feeling unprotected without their frames. The parents felt that the moment had finally come for them to withdraw. They had passed along all their knowledge to their children, and could finally move on to the second part of Mr. G's plan. The time had come for them to turn into slugs... The parents knew that they now had to substantiate all they had taught their children through their own shining example. To put their empty words into practice. Their bodies ossified, they knew that true penitence would only come when they slowly began to crawl across the earth, praying God to forgive them for the arrogance that had taken hold of them. They began to withdraw from the city streets into the woods besides the road, where it was easier to crawl along the wet ground. Like their framed children, it was initially quite hard for them; their knees and cheeks were bloody, and their mouths full of dirt. At first, they could only stand an hour before returning, dead tired, to the comfortable sofas in their houses, while their children ran tearfully about them, begging them to stop with the experiment — they had proven that they were serious, it didn't matter that people in their generation weren't all the same height! In the end, the children would have preferred to have happy parents, or to have parents altogether, rather than live according to rules defined by ideology. At one point, they got the urge to rip the frames from themselves, but they no longer could as they had become a part of their bodies! The children would throw themselves on their beds and slumber tearfully until the next morning, which brought the hope that things would take a turn for the better... As their parents' difficult years of accommodating to their new bodies passed, they began to spend more and more time out of the house. They would only miss lunch at first, but soon they weren't there for dinner either, until one day they no longer even slept in the house. Their children would run into them on rainy days along some trail, stretching long and slimy with their heads on the ground. All their bodies looked like one another. All similar height and with invisible faces lost in the earth, the children couldn't know which of them were their parents, if it even mattered anymore. The children would be happy that everything was finally going as it should, they would pat whoever's parents on their slimy backs and continue along their way. It seemed that the country was functioning better and better — now, all the people on the street were more or less the same height — some even no longer needed to wear their frames — while the older generation spent their lives in the wilderness on the roadsides, turned into horizontal backs whose insignificant differences in height could be tolerated. The dear children in the city even built a few slippery pavements just for them, so the parents could visit and remember their homes and their past lives in the city. Life in the country became exactly as they had wanted it. The government, by then composed of new, framed generations, nominated Mr. G for president, but they couldn't manage to find him... Why, how could they have forgotten — he was surely one of the shiniest slugs in the brush by now! They made do with a statue of him with the body of a slug and a human head, which they placed on the main square before going on with their lives. The happy framed children couldn't have known about the changes that had been going on in the meantime in the hidden world behind the bushes. At the point when their parents finally adapted to their crawling bodies, whose height was no longer equal to their length, and whose entire mass pressed against the earth instead of simply the soles of their feet, their perception changed completely! Because their new way of moving about was so slow, they reached a level on which movement was equivalent to standing still, which led them to a higher state of being. As if they themselves had become gravity. They no longer gravitated towards anything, nor did they know of goals. Every part of their bodies was there where it was, at a physically different centimetre from other parts of their bodies, but together they formed a harmony of difference, a wholeness of motion and stillness. Each part of their bodies felt a different colour, a different sound, a different word... They felt that goals as such didn't exist, because their front was always in front of their middle, and it could in no way feel the same things as their middle, because what the front had already passed the middle was yet to experience. Their new bodies helped them develop into much more complex personalities, into people who seemed to be composed of many souls but who still functioned in harmony. Man now seemed a primitive creature whose curse was that he felt the only source of thought throughout his life to be his head, which was never in contact with the ground. The head, that pinnacle of the body in disaccord with the rest, forces him to constantly strive for something. For, in the end, man's body is simply in the wrong position, and thus his mind is as well. His entire body touches the Earth when he dreams, and he even calls his dreams "dreams," considering them unreal and untrue, when that is actually the true life he should be working to develop, that horizontal position…! If they could only explain this now to their framed children. But, sadly, there was no longer a way to do this, and so the parents had to forget their former lives, which now seemed false and strange. They let go of the entire past within them and decided never again to point their heads at anything except themselves. They wouldn't "go" anywhere anymore. They would only move in a circle, their tops facing their tops, until they finally met and disappeared. And that is how it came to pass. Only some chose to keep exclusively to the ground, while others began to bend their tops into the air until they finally connected with themselves somewhere beneath the sky. The latter simply disappeared, while the former left behind circular paths on the ground. After a few months, wild, disorderly grass began to grow there. All of a sudden, the entire country was full of grassy paths no one could get rid of. The grass grew like mad, wherever it felt like growing. The framed children had no idea what to do with the grass, and they hadn't the faintest where their parents were. They decided to abandon their country, but unfortunately they couldn't survive anywhere else, because other countries weren't designed for framed people. The final survivor wrote an appeal calling for Mr. G to be arrested. Mr. G, who had secretly found his inspiration in a spiral labyrinth of wild roses, was accused of the worst genocide in history. They never found him — neither him, nor his country. Today, its location has been long forgotten… It could be absolutely any lowland on Earth, free of hill and valley.

WEIWEI

Weiwei sits at the table and eats. She eats bite by bite, and there is always a space between each bite. Weiwei is generally full of spaces, spaces, like the Japanese are, maybe. "Ma," as Shakiro used to say, "Ma." A silence of words. Weiwei says it too, although she isn't from Japan... I could never be like Weiwei. I watch her. It's as if she thinks about every bite she slowly brings to her mouth, imperceptibly, as if the emptiness of her mouth naturally continues into the air through which her hand and the fork she holds in it are passing, as if there is no bodily barrier between them. Her face pulls into an unconscious, negligible grimace, and remains tense, frozen in the moment. Who knows what she's thinking, it doesn't matter what she's thinking. It's nice to watch her eat. As she eats, she says: "I read something today that I wrote when I was twenty. I asked myself, wow, who is that girl? It was, rather good. You know, the energy of youth." Weiwei often stretches out the syllables at the ends of her sentences, or adds a "yeah" in a low-falling tone. She then begins to laugh loudly, from the heart, perhaps even with a dose of childish innocence. I don't know much about Weiwei. I know she only socialises at dinnertime. I usually see her in the kitchen and I'm never sure if she feels like talking, so I don't want to keep her for too long. She usually takes the food she makes into her room, and when I cross the terrace I see her through the window eating at her computer. I find it strange, people usually don't like eating alone — perhaps she enjoys it because she's thinking about each bite? She seems to have some kind of different relationship towards food. But one thing remains a fact, and that is that she can't make food in her room, although she would certainly like to, and so I interrogate her a bit as she bangs frying pans about the cooker. I discover that she lived in London for three years, that she published a novel the title of which is unfamiliar to me, and that she is currently "happy with her life". Soon, the meal is done, and Weiwei leaves the kitchen. After that, I don't see Weiwei for two days. I imagine her sitting on the bed in her room which consists only of a table and a bed, looking at the space in front of her with her black eyes. And so on for hours, until she goes to the kitchen to put water on for tea. I'm sure Weiwei can stare at the space in front of herself for hours. And so I think of Weiwei, I think in motion as I ride my bicycle through the uncut grass. It's nice to think of Weiwei while moving. The birds are loud and discordant, and the cotton of dandelions flies through the air. The day hatches in all its fullness, not a single part remains hidden beneath the earth or the clouds. Today is separated from death by the greatest number of light years.

The next day, I meet Weiwei again as she's eating dinner. She's eating slowly again, although she does wolf down a few bites, and it's impossible to imagine how so much food can fit in such a small, narrow body. Again, I consider that it might be because Weiwei thinks as she eats. Her thoughts burn calories during each bite. It's a bit like you wrote me once, that sticky words cling to the squares and facades; we people and things age because of a patina of words... And so perhaps Weiwei is disappearing rapidly, just like the narrator in her story, who her character Ouyang thinks is going to disappear... Eating, this time, Weiwei informs us that her family is coming to visit her. I imagine her parents arriving, thin and buried in luggage... She says — calmly, because it's implied — that her husband and son are coming. I would never have said that she had a husband and son, but there it is — Weiwei has suddenly become a mother. Just a sentence or two after the one in which she used to live in London and was happy with her life. And then she emits two, three long 'ma's, filled with the rustling of willow branches beside a bridge on a green river. The willows now stand before a rain that will never come. It is dusk, the sky is purplish-blue, the sight demands many words. A trip to the epicentre, a pairing. Weiwei isn't on the terrace, nor is she in her room. She's gone, she's off in the woods somewhere listening to a long-forgotten human tongue similar to the sighing of those long stalks growing out of the tree's scalp. Her rare words are finally equivalent to the wind, like the emptiness of her mouth with all the air in the universe around it. Language and wind finally become a single, unitary rushing of air... We others head back to the warm house, close the door, and pour red wine in the silence of a room in which each word is heavy furniture we clumsily move from place to place to make ourselves feel "cosy". Just for a moment, the words connect in the gaps between themselves, we forget where we are, and the conversation is light. Maybe this happens only when we talk about language itself, only then does language pull us into itself completely. Like the forest pulled Weiwei in.

I cross the terrace the next day again, and she truly still isn't there. She isn't in her room, nor is she making breakfast in the kitchen. I see her walking past a row of white cows, all staring in her direction, and I see her lying on a field full of tiny, yellow flowers. The others tell me she's gone sightseeing with her family. She's coming back in a day or two. Now she's carrying her tiny child on her shoulders, a child that laughs just like his mother. Her child is her best friend, I think. Soon his arm will grow thicker than his mother.

Two days later, Weiwei is back at dinner. She sits across from me like every day. Silence reigns around her, except for the bell-like laughter that often comes out of the emptiness of her mouth, similar to the rustling of the trees, the ambiguity of an archaic language balancing on the edge of metamorphosis. Dusk, says Weiwei. Dusk. I wanted a child very much, but it's difficult having a child, you don't have time for anything at the start… She continues eating as if each bite is an entire world in time. We had known each other only briefly and I decided to get pregnant. I see her large stomach outgrowing her entirely, her arms and legs become tiny and imperceptible in it. Her stomach carries her off into the sky, a stomach different from all other stomachs, as light as a balloon. Then I see her, thin and without a stomach, sitting and reading a book, and her whole pregnancy is taking place in the fingers she is using to hold the book. Before him, I was in a relationship for eight years, with a woman, she says. Until I met him, I was only with women. But, actually, it's the same to be with a woman and with a man. She begins laughing again, that loud laugh that exposes a bit of her gums, which seems to represent everything light for her being, the outside world in which she sometimes decides to open herself, open herself with her child, and then withdraw again into her room like a snail and stare at the empty space in front of her for hours.

After dinner, we walk through the woods. The trail is wide and white, it seems like the last remnant of the day amidst the falling dark. At the end of this curve, in the distance, I see a dark tree, an entrance into a mystical tunnel that will encompass us entirely. Along the path, Weiwei avoids the bare, convoluted slugs, snails freed of their shells. She is afraid of stepping on their brilliant, black bodies, and so she screams every once in a while. I tell her that I went walking here one day after the rain, and that the slugs reminded me of art. I stopped above each small body and observed them for a few moments. Maybe those slugs were to me like the bites she brings to her mouth so slowly that the very act of her eating is completely invisible…

We walk on. We hear loud movement in the tall grass beside the path. We can't see what it is, we can only hear it moving. Out of the waves of grass whose colour has been sucked up by the dusk, a stag, a man, a wild boar might appear. But the blades simply continue rustling… That archaic language again. A language portending an image. A language of uncertainty… The French have an expression for dusk. *Entre chien et loup.* Between the dog and the wolf. Before the wolf attacks the farm at night. Before the wolfhound turns back into a wolf… Yes, she just used that phrase today in a story she's writing. To Weiwei, this expression is Mandarin, not French. Dusk is always more sorrowful in coastal towns, although we're not sure why. We slowly begin heading home, the sky above the bridge shows the last iota of purple. The contours of the green fence dwindle into the night. I'm inspired, says Weiwei. I'm inspired, I say. Perhaps it isn't youth, that energy, Weiwei. Maybe it's when we get caught up in someone's spirit, then we can write like that. We enter the kitchen to the hooting of owls and close the door to the room. Weiwei puts a kettle on for tea. Weiwei is always drinking tea, I've noticed. We take a few sips together.

Socks

He and I were a *pair* (*Old French* paire ← *Latin* par: equal)
in the true sense of the word. *Two equal objects or two people
who usually go together or work together...* One and the other,
like a left and right leg, we could always be seen together. We
walked through town together, melted into the passers-by,
poured into the crowd... He was always hurrying somewhere,
but whenever he would set foot on the street without a particular goal before him, he would start to walk slowly, observing
everything around him. In those moments, he seemed older,
almost like an old man leaning both palms against his back...
And the time would become some other time, too... Carriages
rolled along the streets and the Art Nouveau facades were brand
new... We could also be seen in the specially marked depart-
ments of the modern city... Together at the "market", we
bought fluorescent vegetables suffocated in thin, plastic bags...
After the "theatre", we argued because I always commented
more on the film than he did, which he found irritating, as did
I... You could find us at the "sauna", where artificial waterfalls
fell roughly on our backs... And in various "cafés" where we
would drink beer after work, imagining some new, entirely
possible life stories... Yes, even the drivers could have easily
begun waving at us from their cars as we rushed past them on
our scooter on the way to work. There, our paths would finally
diverge, as each of us would slam the door to our own office.
Only the wall between them separated our days, because by
evening, we would be sleeping in the same bed within the same
walls... Breathing under the blanket of communal privacy, two

people in one bed in one room. A *pair*, two people who *have one function or comprise a whole...* Our function was the same, because even though we had different jobs, we also invested our energy in the same company for a while, and our unity could be best seen at night, when our two sleeping bodies would embody a scene together on the canvas of our bed. For a time, before we knew each other thoroughly, our life flowed more-or-less idyllically. But one day, on the mattress leaning on the wall in the guest room, freshly-washed socks began to appear. They were tossed on the mattress like half-dead, gasping fish... Just a few centimetres apart from each other. They seemed a bit lost in the world of chaos they themselves had created. Ordinary monotone socks beside those with flowers of various sizes, striped ones, variations on the monotone (thick, thin, lacy, woollen, ones with a thick hem, ones with a thin hem, ones with logos, and ones without), and then socks with holes, ankle socks, sporty socks, knee-high socks, white socks... An entire world of playful differences in that modest universe, usually hidden under the trouser-leg, which never even took sides, because who has ever heard of a "left" or "right" sock despite the fact that they spend entire days in "left" or "right" shoes, on "left" or "right" feet?! The lightness of these garments, the simplicity of movement with which they are put on and with which they hug the ankle and foot like little caterpillars... This, and the fact that we don't have to stop and think if a sock is a left or right sock before we put it on, instead doing so without a second thought, gives them a hint of freedom... They come in pairs, and yet they are not limited by the norms of left and right, visible in winter only if whoever wears them decides to make them so, but usually hidden beneath the trousers... All this gave them a dash of identity... At least they had the chance to be what they were... And they gave the person wearing them an opportunity to vent, to express themselves completely — an opportunity for revolution! But despite all of the evidence provided here proving the independence of the sock, some wiseacre had to come along and ruin everything! Some horrible bureaucrat who couldn't see past his own dirty feet concluded that socks had to be stamped with the same pattern and sold in pairs, because there are always two of them, just like there are always two feet! He *paired* them, one might say. Or, better yet — he found a function for them, because function is what makes someone or something a pair. Eros struck them with a striped pattern and created problems for the human race, while freeing socks of their identity and originality! All of a sudden, before putting on their shoes, everyone had to look for a pair of socks that "go together", because without the same socks, they couldn't leave the house. If they didn't have to wear a uniform themselves, they at least had to uniform their feet and ankles, because the existence of a number greater than "one" in our civilisation — such as "two", for example — leads immediately to a tendency towards uniforming. We have to mark ourselves, after all. Recruit ourselves, down there beneath our trouser-legs, where at least our unconscious and our dreams could live in peace! And so this idea, which later nearly became a rule — the idea that two socks must be equal, or something is wrong with the person wearing them — completely changed not only the world, but human consciousness as well. Not only did socks engender terror and general hysteria in cities! People ransacked their entire flats just to find two of the same sock… Because of socks, people were frequently late to work, which caused traffic jams in the streets. Whether a war or a play in the theatre, absolutely nothing could start without looking for a pair of socks. Socks were the prologue to everything public, everything that didn't happen at home. Straight away, left or right, party orientation, politics… the military… up and down! In the house, however, they were lost or just dirty, thrown about the floor… Otherwise, they were never really talked about… Except in our exceptional case. The one and only important thing that happened at home for which socks served as an introduction was our argument! Just for me, my par(tner) decided to exhibit all of our socks on the mattress, innocent victims on the battlefield, in order to prove that he could no longer match any of his socks because of me! The mattress was my courtroom, and I assume that the prosecutor had hoped that I would calmly take the stand and attempt to do the impossible for him — that is, to pair at least some of his socks! However, if the sock refuses, it refuses. Had I wanted with all my heart to pair them, it wouldn't have been possible. I had put on unmatched pairs so many times that particular individuals disappeared without a trace, while we didn't manage to wash others in the same load of wash as their partners! Socks got lost, for one reason or another, in the vortex of the washing machine and the cycle of life. There was no longer a way to bring them back to the imposed structure of existing "in a pair." They became individuals that circled in an orbit around our feet, separately and yet all together… Some never touched the floor, while some happened to touch it more than once. They would stop and feel the Earth beneath them… And then end up once again in the hamper, ready for a new cycle and a new journey. I perceived this as a natural state of being, but my better half went crazy on me and tossed all the socks about the mattress for the very same reason: for him, having two of the same sock on his feet was a natural state of being. To unpair socks, to wear a different sock on each foot, was to rape nature. My beau found this as painful as if someone were twisting his spine, and he could no longer bear the fact that he couldn't find two of the same sock anywhere in the house! In a daze, he mentioned various orderly structures in nature — the structure of crystals, water, molecules, etc. I tried to explain how two socks don't metamorphose into something else when they are together, and that it's not a given that they be together, that there is no need to bring them together in a unified structure. All in vain. The man nearly fell ill from unpaired socks. Although his new side did disappoint me, I still wanted to solve this problem… But he claimed there was no solution, however, because *I* was unable to fight my nature, and that I would destroy the harmony and idyll of every newly bought pair of socks, which would thus wreck the harmony of *his* nature. I was a destructive, chaotic force, he claimed. I was like the wind and like an earthquake, except after me, the earth was not renewed. I was an eternal dark age of chaos, and if I really wanted to, I would have already paired those bloody socks! It seemed to me that he didn't really understand much about life, although he did have a fairly clear picture of me. I would certainly — not out of ill will, but because it was my karma — always unpair all the socks again. *A pair, that which is made equal by a certain characteristic.* This is obviously not what we were. We walked the streets, his socks matching and mine unmatched. And soon, due to our irreconcilable differences, we decided to separate for a time. He went for a while to live with his mother, who not only paired his socks but ironed them as well, and so he calmed down, at least as far as that was concerned. I stayed in our flat and decided to enjoy a little solitude. Now, the unmatched socks reminded me even more of us, and I was reluctant to remove that art exhibition from my flat. They made me feel both sad and happy and nostalgic at the same time… and I didn't feel alone with them. Somehow, they symbolised us, all of our differences and different views on life. Because, although we were a pair for a very long time according to various definitions of that word, we still loved entirely different ways of existing, as was apparent at our peak. Our case made the simple contrasts of which mankind is composed quite clear. *We were a small picture of the world.* A pair. *Man and woman. Engineer and textile designer. Scientist and artistic spirit. Rationality and intuition. Order and chaos.* His job was to produce a "reality" that worked, while my "job" was to "create" myself, because without that creation, I felt as if neither I nor the world existed. My entire life consisted of me convincing myself that we exist, although I didn't always do a very good job of this. Although all the fabric I drew on paper was intended for our bodies and all those clothes were intended for us, the human race, and confirmed our existence, it was in fact composed of gaps that frightened me. First and foremost, the wide gaps through which our limbs only passed — gaps for our arms, legs, and head... Then narrow gaps that wrapped around our fingers, breasts, bottoms, and feet. Sometimes, after I was done with a piece of clothing, I would feel like I was designing clothes for spirits... and that I would never succeed in convincing myself of our existence. My work consisted of an endless number of gaps, and it was only within them, within that space I didn't fill with fabric, that I could see the truth... A mirror for everything, an eternal metamorphosis. The feeling was quite frightening and uncomfortable, on the one hand, but in time I realised that it was only this kind of approach that could free me. Rules like "two of the same socks" or "let tram conductor check ticket" seemed like the promotion of some false reality... But he — he didn't even consider subjects like this until I unpaired all the socks. As if he was afraid of the indecipherable truth implied by two different socks on one's feet... And so he direly wanted to go back to his designed reality of rules to be followed. He held to these forms; he looked up to them, not to my gap-mirrors. And he didn't want to give in. With each passing day, I was more and more surprised that the telephone wasn't ringing, and only bit by bit was it getting through to me that he really never would call me again because of those bloody socks! All of a sudden, the life cycle of the socks I washed began to sadden me — somehow those poor things were no longer dear to me, through no fault of their own. I watched them mixing about unpaired in the washing machine, and now they completely reminded me of us. We had started to live like this, unpaired and circular like my socks, and yet I felt lonely, and none of my well-tested theories could ease my pain. When I would recognise one of his socks, I would pair it with one of mine — I would join them into a many-coloured bundle and put them away in a drawer. I soon noticed that the drawer was getting full, and that I had to call him, regardless of the outcome. He hesitated at first, but finally he came to our flat. As fast as I could, I opened the drawer and showed him the various socks bundled inside. Some were bundled up neatly, into a little ball, such that you could barely see that the outer brown sock hid a yellow one, for example. I had made sculptures out of some of them, bundling them messily, their tentacles sticking out of other socks. All those socks were combinations of his and my socks... I told him that this was a new way of making pairs, opposite from pairing by colour or pattern — instead, by us, as if we were mixing genes. My sock and his, interwoven, comfortably fulfilled, without a gap between them. He stared wordlessly at those two socks for a time, and then, suddenly and a bit violently, took them into his hands and pulled them apart. He threw a white sock on the floor, and a black sock flew under the desk. I, also wordlessly, picked up one first and then the other off the floor, and then I slowly pulled them, a black sock and a white sock, over my bare feet. With a loving look, I told him that this was us, those two socks on my feet. For the next few moments, I just stood there motionless, a fragile being offering itself whole for him to observe. He then ran to the dryer and wildly threw all the socks on the floor. I knew he was looking for a needle in a haystack, a sock he would manage to pair with one of the socks on my feet. It all reminded me of some kind of strange, twisted, tragicomic version of Cinderella... Not a moment had passed before the prince ripped the white sock from my foot and theatrically took off his shoes, and then his socks as well. With a dramatic motion, he put a white sock on his right foot, and another white sock, which he had miraculously managed to find amidst that jumble of laundry, on his left foot. They shone whitely, paired, on his feet. We stood opposite one another for a while, as if preparing for a duel, him with two white socks on his feet, and I with one bare foot and one black sock. The prince finally said that this was "Him", those two same socks on his very own feet, and I, looking at my feet, answered that I thought more within the concept of "Us"... At this sentence, he merely looked at me disappointedly and slowly, robust and mute, strolled out of my house. Like a lost puppy, my left foot remained bare and abandoned. I threw myself on the bed and began to cry. I was filled with an immense feeling of emptiness I didn't know how to fill, and my years of experience in design had taught me that filling gaps never solves anything, anyhow... Cinderella's prince had it easy — the only thing he had to do was to seal the emptiness of a found shoe with a small foot. They didn't have to go any further than that... And, luckily for them, Cinderella was a real woman — and always wore stockings.

Flyers

I got off the train at the airport station, and again, I was struck by the unusual feeling that I hadn't changed places since I left home. At first, the train station had looked like a street, but now the airport looked like a train station. My invisible, private gondola had delivered me to a box of an airport that could take me to any number of other places. Only escalators, halls, and a few *movators, travelators, autowalks* repeating the sentence *"mind your step, mind your step"* in resigned female voices separated me from Tenerife, Geneva, Shanghai, Linköping, Pisa, Tel Aviv, Madrid, Ljubljana, Prague, Istanbul, Moscow, Rome… It all seemed too easy, as if my body were nothing more than light fabric hung on a wire hooked onto the window of my house, a wire that led throughout the entire world. I watched people flying speedily about the airport as if they didn't need an *autowalk*, let alone an airplane. I had to keep pace with them, because it felt like the merry-go-round of bodies lit by flashing adverts would make me sick if I stopped. I paused only for a second, trying to concentrate on *Arrivals I* while the people around me came and went, disappearing in yawns of air. *Arrivals* was to the left, I concluded after reading the sign, and headed that way, although *Arrivals* looked exactly the same as *Departures*. Every direction looked the same, even though they all led to opposite hemispheres of the Earth; we airport people all looked the same, as well, whether travellers, airport employees, or simply people waiting. We were simultaneously going somewhere and staying put, up until the moment when some of us actually took off or went home… On the one hand, this place made us bodiless and free, enriched with the prospects of daydreaming, and on the other, it made us material, dependent on fragile paper, money, and passports. Walking, out of the corner of my eye, I noticed that *Arrivals I* was surrounded by people, some of whom held papers with names written on them. It's a special feeling, to wait for someone you've never seen for any reason whatsoever... To pair them with a piece of paper. To crumple it under your fingers after you pat them on the back. To replace cellulose with meat... I don't need a paper like that, because I've known the person I'm supposed to meet for a whole eternity. She's a friend who is finally coming to visit me... Bubbly as always, as if I'd just seen her yesterday. We'll greet each other as if we really had seen each other yesterday, but the way she says "Hi" will give her away. She'll mumble the greeting somewhat under her breath, but there will be something significant in it. As if her "Hi" quivered a bit somewhere in the middle. That's how she always greets me when we haven't seen each other for a while. Who knows how I greet her, and how she realises that I'm happy to see her...

I sit in the café right across from *Arrivals I* and I begin to observe the faces that emerge from the double sliding doors. Soon, I'll see a familiar face with lines dear to me... She's about to show up, any moment now... The sliding doors open and close, open, close, but my friend isn't there. People well up ceaselessly, carried by a wild tide from all ends of the Earth. The doors open, close, open, close, there's not a moment for them to catch their breath. The doors count time in grains of faces lost in thought... It's beginning to seem strange to me, especially because of the empty baggage carousel I see through the glass walls. I also notice that all the people with papers in their hands are still standing around the improvised hallway through which arriving travellers should be exiting. It seems to me that nearly no one has left with the traveller they were waiting for. Perhaps just a few of them. I decide to ask what's happening, just in case... A woman with too much gel in her hair is sitting at the information desk. Her nails are red.

"Excuse me, can you confirm that flight SK 9301 really has landed, like it says on the screen?" I ask resignedly through the glass, as if she weren't there, as if she were a dictaphone for giving information instead of a person.

"Yes, miss, the plane has landed," she answers with a smile. "All the passengers from that flight left the baggage area quite some time ago."

"Do you have my friend V.S. on the list?" I asked, somewhat concerned by now.

"Yes, miss. Your friend landed today at exactly 3:45 PM."

"But I've been waiting for her for some time now at *Arrivals I*, and I haven't seen hide or hair of her!"

"In that case, please try calling her or go back to *Arrivals I* and check again. I'm sure you'll find her soon."

"Alright. Thank you very much. I'm really not sure what's going on," I mumbled through my teeth, and continued wandering frantically about the airport.

First, I went back to *Arrivals I*. All those people were still standing there with their papers with names on them. Now they somehow looked as if they had been rained on, both they and their papers. They had no idea what was going on either, and they shrugged at my questions. They just kept on standing there, because hope dies last. But the hallway the eagerly awaited stars were supposed to be walking down was completely empty, as if the airport were closed. The movement of passengers had calmed down also, making it seem as if all the hubbub and commotion had suddenly stopped. As if this modern world was only able to stand still in moments of doubt, misfortune, or insecurity. The sequence would only last long if someone else, or some higher power, commanded it to. No one was strong enough anymore to decide for themselves about standing. Because no one, and I mean no one, wanted to wait anymore. Not for a moment, let alone this long! Some people, to my great surprise, had slowly begun heading home without having met their friends or business partners. It was obviously the end of times! The situation, they were sure, would get cleared up very soon… Nothing bad had happened, the plane hadn't crashed, there were no terrorists nearby… The plane had continued on to its following destination in perfect working order… The fact that the people had vanished like undelivered text messages was entirely normal to this group of waiting people. What mattered was that the norms according to which we were taught to live showed no trace of abnormality… I continued my search, moving from one traveller to another, from one official to another… But I simply couldn't manage to reach the top of the pyramid, the person who could answer the question of what had happened to my friend. They all, naturally, stared at me in confusion and asked me the same questions. Did the plane land? Has the luggage been collected? Have I received a disturbing phone call that might point to something actually having happened to my friend? As the answers to these questions were "yes," "yes," "no," then why was I looking for my friend at the airport at all instead of calling her? They would only redirect me to some other official, not paying any mind to my complaint that my friend's phone had been off for hours, that her voice had disappeared along with the rest of her… Each new official would do the same, and I don't know how long I would have run around in circles had I not finally run into an official who thought me mad because I attacked him before he even had a chance to open his mouth. He told me to calm down, and that he had already prepared everything for me. He was, no more no less, the official who had been charged with communicating with us, the people waiting for flight SK 9301.

He stood there at the foot of the pyramid, proud of his title, unaware of the fact that his colleagues not only didn't respect him, but weren't even aware of his existence. Lost in a sea of travellers and other airport officials, here he was — "Manager of the Lost, Found, and Pending."

"Don't worry about a thing, miss. Your friend has arrived safe and sound," he told me, thrilled at the fact that not everyone who had been waiting had gone home.

"And where has she been until now, if I might ask? Has she ended up in jail? I've been looking for her for hours... First, all of your colleagues look at me as if I'm crazy for even looking for her. And now, after this whole wild goose chase, you're giving me strange looks because I don't believe you when you say you've found her."

"Please be patient for just a few minutes and I'll deliver her to you," he says kindly, as if he is running the show.

"You'll deliver her to me? Oh, thank you so much, please do..." I answer, ironically but with a tinge of hope in my voice, before slumping onto a nearby chair.

No more than a few minutes had passed before he called me over and coldly handed me an envelope. A lump stuck in my throat as I suddenly imagined something bad had happened to my friend. A telegram never brings good news... But the official smiled reassuringly, encouraging me to open the letter. Now I was sure it was a letter my friend had written, explaining something humorous about the whole situation. I must admit that, if only for a hundredth of a second, I was deeply happy to have received a letter written in her hand, — something I hadn't experienced for a long time — instead of her herself... A letter scented by the skin of my friend's palm as it moved slowly towards the right-hand side of the paper, in harmony with each letter that blossomed beneath it... But, when I finally opened it, I saw that the only trace of my friend was her signature. The official was still smiling at me approvingly, and I began to read the following:

PERSONAL INFORMATION ABOUT THE PASSENGER
First and last name: V.S.
Place of residence: Skalinska street, 10000 Zagreb, Croatia
Passport number: 00009897390627
Age: 32
Height: 163.5 cm
Weight: 53 kg

TRIP INFORMATION
Length of stay: 6 days
Dates of stay: 6, 7, 8, 9, 10, 11 April 2014
Place of residence during stay: Flat of V.L., Street of Fleeting Thoughts, 20000
Cultural monuments to be visited by the passenger during the stay: Passenger's choice

RECORDING OF PASSENGER
Description of head and face: Normal sized skull, which falls into the category of normal sized skulls. Blonde, wavy hair that covers nearly the entire back. Small, bluish eyes. Oval face, the skin of which falls into the category of medium-thin. The individual will thus not have many wrinkles in the future. Cheeks are ruddy, and lips are reddish. Smile is regular and warm, and reveals orderly rows of teeth. Neck is normal in size, neither too long nor too short.
Visual description of body: Well-proportioned body. Calves are neither too thick nor too thin. Firm breasts. Arms of normal length that end in hands falling into the category of small hands.

Description of voice: Loud speech. Somewhat shrill in moments of anger. Production of large quantities of words. Voice otherwise pleasant in tone.
Description of gesticulation: Frequent waving of hands. Relaxed demeanour.

At this point, the Flyer ended. Only the date and signature of my friend and the signature of an official stood in the lower left-hand corner. There was a bar code in the right-hand corner. I was truly confused. What the devil was this? The *Meta-Form* of V.S.?!

"Excuse me, could you be so kind as to explain what this is about?" I asked the still-smiling Manager of the Lost, Found, and Pending.

"Ah, you don't know?" His expression darkened suddenly. "Perhaps that makes sense, this is a new law, and as you don't speak the language of the country you live in, it's easy to miss out on news... In short... No, wait, let me ask you first..." He scratched his head and paused for a moment. "Are you familiar with the airport security system, all those machines a traveller has to pass through in order to finally enter the Duty Free zone?"

I nodded impatiently at his chatting, which seemed like it was going to last a while. He was going to explain everything up, down, and lengthwise... He had the time... The airport surely had around a hundred such managers so that each of them could devote quality time to their confused customers. I would probably find out where my friend was a few hours from now.

"Those machines are becoming more and more sensitive," he continued calmly, as if I weren't there. "Now, for example, they can see how much water a passenger is carrying within their body." He shrugged as if this were all implied.

"What does that mean, then? Before, you couldn't bring a bottle of water with you because of the risk of liquid explosives, and now we can't even bring ourselves? You must be joking!" I snapped at him... I also noticed that my anger betrayed something feigned. I wasn't really angry, because I had expected something like this. In fact, I could hardly wait for something like this to happen! In a way, I was even morbidly looking forward to the next idea from the distorted world we live in. A world in which mucus isn't slimy and beings are born in glass, fluorescent boxes. The world has always been grotesque, but its grotesqueness has never been this clinical.

"Well, I think you've got it right. It seems that people who are more than 63% water by weight (except for children, who always have a higher percentage of water by weight than adults) are a potential danger to our society. First and foremost — and I don't know how to explain this scientifically — but they could somehow hide a liquid explosive in their bodies, because they have excess water within them. A special operation could make a little 'pocket' in their bodies, a small container full of their own water, where they could hide a liquid explosive. And then they get on a plane, and boom! No more plane...! There was already a case like that in the newspapers, I don't know if you saw that article... A really tricky thing. What people won't think of to bring harm to others... In the end, though, water is a symbol of life and birth, but them? BOOM! The apocalypse!" He watched me with interest, even anticipating my approval.

"No, I didn't see that article. Nor did I know that something like 'extra water' existed in our bodies, or that it could be put to such good use..." I looked at him, annoyed, as if he, the poor fool, foundandlost manager, or how did it go? Manager of the unresolved? He's to blame for everything. What could the poor guy do? Stupid situations like this put bread on his table. But I was still upset. "If you might be so kind, would you please explain what other reasons there might be to prevent such people from crossing the holy border?"

"Another reason..." He began to explain, proud that he was doing his job so well... "Another reason is that there are theories — albeit unproven theories — that people who carry more water than the majority of the population are quite likely more fertile than others. There is also a much greater chance that these people will have twins, which is definitely not in our country's interests. We don't have room for any more immigrants, and every traveller is a potential danger as far as that is concerned. Maybe a traveller turns into an illegal immigrant. This country is already too full of all sorts of people..." he said plainly, not devoting an iota of attention to the fact that I was also a foreigner.

"Fine," I said, not wanting to start a discussion about immigrants. "Now that you've expounded all your reasons, might you finally explain where my friend is? Is she going to finally show up, or is she one of those people potentially dangerous to society who aren't let across the border?" I waved the Flyer with her signature in his face.

"Well, believe it or not, your friend will do both. Our orderly society does in fact care for human rights, so some smart guy up there on top found a way to sit in two chairs simultaneously — or, even better, to be in two different places and times at the same time!" He was so astonished by this extraordinary discovery that he went quiet and stared off into space for a few moments. "Your friend was truly too 'watery' to be allowed across the border," he continued pregnantly in a low, descending tone. "This is why she was brought across as the Meta-Form of V.S., which is equivalent to her original, meaty, still-extant form. In other words, the Meta-Form of V.S. is, in fact, your friend!" he revealed to me pridefully without so much as a blink, as if he were showing me America for the first time.

There was nothing left for me to do at that point other than burst out laughing.

"Hahahahahahahahahahahaha! This miserable little piece of paper is my friend?! Oh, the poor thing, look what's become of her! Should I set her on fire and put her in an urn?" I told him, clutching at my stomach.

"No, you're not understanding me," he said, somewhat insulted. "This, as you call it, 'little piece of paper' is, in fact, your living friend."

"Living? Oh, well, even better! Should I hug her, or what? You have truly lost your mind!" I suddenly switched from amusement back to anger. "Are you crazy?!" I began screaming. "What is wrong with you?! This Flyer, my friend?! This is beyond insane! If someone had told me that I would have to talk to someone about something like this one day, I would have said they were deranged! I thought the difference between People and Paper was as clear as day, unless we're living in some kind of hallucinogenic area! What is wrong with you? I'm leaving! Those people who left a few hours ago really were the smart ones. If my friend is Paper, then I'm a Hippopotamus, and you're — oh, I don't know, a Teapot! Is it just you with Alzheimer's disease, or is it this entire society?! Dear God, what is wrong with you...? My friend, the Flyer."

"Yes, and she flew straight here to you! Instead of being happy, you're off making scenes around the airport." He looked about, wagging his head.

"Oh, please, stop trying to sell me these stories! Is there a hidden camera somewhere around here or what?!" I couldn't believe something like this was happening. They had finally managed to upset me. With his idiocy and their insanity... But, at the word "Story", he suddenly got serious.

"Do not, please, mention the word *story!*" he suddenly began yelling at me. "I'm talking about serious things here. The word *story* — look it up in the dictionary — can mean: *1. (a) a verbal account, a telling (b) a brief telling of a historical or imaginary person, event, etc; a fairy tale (c) a short account, such as an artistic creation in prose; a novella 2. rumours, news (usually untrue); a fabrication.* So, I'm not telling you a fairy tale, nor are these old wives tales! This has to do with official, state decisions!" he threatened, pointing to the official stamps that had sealed my friend. "You cannot rip up your friend, because you will end up in jail if you do. You can rip up a book if you like instead, and no one will bat an eye!" he added victoriously. I looked at him, stunned, and whenever I remember that instant, my eyes still bulge in disbelief for a few long, wordless moments. I realised that I no longer had the will to take part in a senseless debate with someone who lived in some other dimension entirely, if you could even call it that. I thanked him resignedly, as if I had just swallowed a valium, and like a robot, my body stiff, I once again melted into the mass of airport people.

Again: *"Mind your step. Mind your step,"* rang under my feet. My friend rustled lightly between my fingers. Painfully reduced, crumpled, dried out. Full of cellulose, glue, and filler. Stiff and hollow. All the water had been sucked out of her. It was unusual — just a few hours ago, I had seen people standing at *Arrivals I* holding papers with the names of people who were soon supposed to appear before them. Now, it seemed like that scene had happened in some entirely different, opposite time... I looked for the word *Exit* so I could go calm down in the fresh air and smoke a cigarette. Outside, smokers from every country stood huddled around a narrow ashtray. I moved away from them a bit and started making a paper airplane out of my friend. No one could take that from me, or at least I hoped not. Forbidding transformation — it was a real miracle they hadn't thought of that yet! If they could transform my friend, I would transform her too. Soon, I was joined by two young

English boys, and we passed the airplane between each other in a circle. I told them it was my friend, at which they shot me confused looks. Somehow, it was hard for them to accept that fact… We played for a short time longer until I felt it was time to leave. I left them the stamped paper airplane as an heirloom, even at the cost of prison time — how was I to forbid the children from playing? And I'm sure my friend would have liked that — being a fragile little airplane in the hands of children, while real metal birds land and take off around you…

After this episode, I headed to the ticket counter, firm in my desire to try and take off today. Not to wait a moment longer. To meet my friend halfway… to meet something… hoping for a fracas at security. As I approached the plastic boxes in which you have to put all your belongings, a discomfort took hold of me that made my breath catch in my throat. I frantically started searching through my pockets to make sure I didn't have something dangerous with me, like tweezers, or an old bullet casing. You never know, you never know — I checked all the openings on my clothes and bags in a panic… But, how to reach into my insides, how to know if too much water is hiding there, in my body…? Finally, my turn came. The plastic Arches awaited me, and there stood Charon, pondering my status. Would he ferry me across the river or not? I snuck through the arch with a quick step, and to my great surprise, I made it through! Silence ruled around me. An ominous "beep" stuck in the scanner's throat… Moments later, I handed my passport to the official, and I very nearly asked him if it perhaps reminded him of my (stamped and sealed) friend. I bit my tongue at the last moment, and with a forced smile, I managed to get past this obstacle as well. Twenty-odd minutes later, I was on the plane buckling my seatbelt. I, it appears, do not have dangerous amounts of water in me, and so there's no need to transform me into paper. I already am paper, just as I am… Nothing more than a thin piece of paper hung on a wire hooked to the window of my house, a wire running through a uniform world. A world in which airports look like streets, streets look like the insides of airplanes, and only the sky exists as a separate entity with no connection to anything else.

The airplane began to take off, and in the blink of an eye, we had ascended above the clouds. We, the chosen ones without too much water inside us, had elevated ourselves above everything. However, here in this new world, I wasn't sure whether we people of meat could consider ourselves living, or if it was merely my reflection, my soul, that was hurtling through the sky in a metal bird.

The Endless Ending

One morning, people in the northern hemisphere were waking up, while people in the southern hemisphere were just finishing their evening's work. Even though the light above all earthly people was completely different, even though completely different words came out of their oral cavities and moved into the empty sky, the people in both hemispheres noticed that there was no water in their taps. That day, the northerners didn't manage to shower before work, and that same night, the southerners went to bed dirty. None of this would have worried them too much had the same situation not repeated the following day. Soon, a rumour spread round the Earth — there was no more water, and not just in Africa! Panic took hold; people began licking the dry corners of their mouths. Never before on Earth had so many slimy human tongues come out of their mouths at the same time, like worms before the rain. But not even the raindrops that rang out on the gutters in rhythm with the clinking of glasses in the nearby restaurant — not even those raindrops were there anymore! The rivers had disappeared without a trace, the seas had flown off on the backs of snowflakes to some unearthly place. 'Drop' nearly disappeared from the dictionary. As if they had just awoken from some foggy dream, only when they began listing madly through dictionaries of all manner of language, only when under A, B, C, D, they failed to find the word "drop" — only then did they realise they were still alive, that their mouths weren't too dry, and that the planet wasn't even overly hot. A cry of happiness rung out across the world in unison: Woohoo!

Yeah! Aaaaaaa! Some even began running various marathons the world over, just to prove that they wouldn't get the least bit sweaty! Everything was somehow easier — they no longer had to carry the weight of water in their guts, and they burned calories with unbelievable speed. Everyone began eating much more and feeling lighter and thinner. Even though all food now tasted like dry biscuits, they continued living as if water had never existed, as if every day were their last. But after some time, they realised that no day had been anyone's last! At least so far. All those people, all of us — and it happened two hundred forty-seven years ago according to the old system of measuring time — we're all still alive! We age, we all look like Methuselah, but we're not dying. We all dig through the Old Testament to find proof that the world was without water for any significant period of biblical time, because if the book is to be trusted, many of the prophets lived for centuries. If we could prove this, we would know that it is possible to bring water back to Earth. Gabriel Garcia Marquez is here with us; many people knock on his door thinking he might know something, because it rained for years in *One Hundred Years of Solitude*. But he just shrugs and continues writing a novel in which the entire plot unfolds under the sea... He points us to Adam and Eve, because if we assume there was no water on Earth until their time, who else could we blame for it coming back? This is all entirely logical, but how to prove it? And how to bring the water back to Earth once you have... It's hard to find the reason why it disappeared, but even harder to call it back, at least until enough time has passed and we've gained enough experience. This is a completely new situation for humankind. We don't know what might happen, or if we'll even survive. Because not a single child, not a single girl, not a single middle-aged man looks with us to the sky. A million hale and hearty old folk look to the sky with sad eyes... We can't come to terms with the idea that we might be the only ones left, that we might even be immortal; there is no more birth, no youth, no hateful old folks' homes. We have to take care of this world, because it's the only thing that keeps us going, but we'd all rather jump into the sea that is no longer there, vanish into its depths. All of us, just like Marquez, have been shrugging impotently for years. Only one philosopher thinks he knows the answer, but let's hope to god he's not right. If he is, it means we're all stuck in eternal limbo. That means that this is hell, a punishment. An endless ending. But a true ending, unfortunately, can only be endless, because all endings were once open-ended, and were followed by beginnings, except in films, which force signed and sealed endings. True endings didn't exist before! If this changeless state continues for centuries to come, then we'll be able to say we've reached the "era of the endless ending", claims the pessimistic philosopher. How to prove this, we all ask ourselves... By forcing every old man and old woman on the planet to think back to the morning or night two hundred and forty-seven years ago, just before they were to discover that there was no water in their taps, and remember if they were happy and satisfied. If all the old folk on Earth answer yes (and there will be no lying — we have very precise lie detectors today!), then his theory is proven. Scientists can continue studying the Old Testament, trying to prove that Eve brought water back to Earth, but according to him, the debate ends here. In the moment when everyone on Earth became satisfied, desire disappeared... All those rains, all those seas, all those rivers — they were all the desire of unborn beings to appear on Earth in solid form. All those waterfalls — perhaps they best illustrate the claim — are the screams of beings who had just felt their first desire to come to life, who were balanced on the cusp of life and non-existence. Every time a child, a cat, a lizard, a rose grew, somewhere in the world, a drop of water would evaporate as if someone had drunk it up. But we living organisms were never satisfied, we always lusted after one another, or after something else, and so the water would always fall back to Earth in the form of rain. This cycle continued for years until we reached an advanced state of development and lost our thirst, exactly two hundred and forty-seven years ago. We can only hopelessly hope, says the pessimistic philosopher, that one morning, we in the northern hemisphere will wake up from our night's sleep, and those in the southern hemisphere from their afternoon nap, and feel an immeasurable thirst. Still half asleep, we'll rush to our taps and drink, drink ourselves to death.

The Sea

Sometimes stories are born when I tell them to you.

Today, she begged to go to the seaside. Today. Just like yesterday. The sea. Through glass windows. Through the treetops. A pencil. Natural in the fingers. A pencil, the centre of an orbit.

Photographs and photographs float around her. And then clouds. Photographs. Through a handwriting of diluted clouds. I love you. She tells the photographs. I love you. Hard-drawn black-and-white faces. In hard-drawn lenses, the reflections of clouds. She's happiest when they fade away. Then the faces are brilliant and trembling, like bodies in motion through a window. Because reflection-memories are more constant than clouds… She, just like humanity, believes that contours are permanent, at least on photo paper. She feels the ground beneath her soles, and that's why it's so. Because a thousand-year-old tree grows out of the ground. Only this makes her keep forgetting about the clouds, as if she never even knew they were there. Forgetfulness was written into the scent of her skin as a child. Just like that sea, the sea, through the fingers with which she slaps our real, meaty, full, aged faces, faces our jaws have graced with form. We today, alive before her (and she before us), are no more than a bottle of Coca Cola from the shop, no more than the stones in an inlet. Paths towards a fulfilled desire. Only the sea is always in the present. Only its waves have no hard edges. Even those bygone trips to the seaside are *now*. Winter in hotels as children where we greeted all the guests at dinner. From table to table, we wished people *bon appétit*, after which we would eat a few crêpes… Have we heard this story…(?), told so many times that it seems it might disappear only if it were carved into stone... That's how some stories are. Hard under the tongue, just like our chins and jaws, just like our true forms, which grandma doesn't see before her.

We are cardboard dolls before her, but it's only in the walls, in the picture frames, that the world multiplies and the world buzzes with summer holidays and fun. The sea is healthy, even for old folk, she told me when I told her it could be bad for her. I said that she couldn't go to the seaside, that she had to stay at home. To cool off? She simply asked in astonishment, and continued watching television. In the afternoon, she asked me again why we shouldn't go to the seaside together. Her daughter won't take her, so her granddaughter will. I told her I wasn't going to the seaside. And again the next day. Again every day. Today. The same as last year. She hasn't been for two years. The sea. The sea. If I won't take her, she'll call her son to take her. He's never let her down. I offer her a Coca Cola and she forgets for a moment. The sea. Coca Cola. The north and south poles of her life.

The next day, my father comes back from the seaside, and she asks him to take her to the seaside. He gives her thirty kuna and takes her to church, and absorbed in the priest's voice, she forgets for a moment. Sunday rings. If he won't take her, she'll call her son to take her! A week later, my brother and mother come back from the seaside. My brother lives with grandma, his girlfriend, and a cat, so she asks him to take her to the seaside every day. She asks him now. To go to the seaside for a swim. He gives her a newspaper, the TV listings for the whole week that comes out on Friday, and she again forgets for a moment. About the sea. Only the pale dusk peers through the windows. And when you were born, just stop me if I've already told you, your grandfather and I were coming back to town from a sailing trip. From the sea! The sea. And me. The North and South Poles of her life.

As if this story were a film exclusively in azure, my father suggests, quick, quick, before summer ends, why don't we all go to the seaside together and put grandma on the waves, under blazing parasols and on steep stairs. The next day, we head off on the old road towards the nearest coastline in a green automobile with a high roof, grandma and all of us together. As we drive, she talks about her grandma and grandpa with whom she lived for a time as a little girl, and they lived at the seaside, and her grandpa wrote a poem for her wedding and she doesn't know where it is now, nor does she remember how it goes exactly. She's sad she lost that poem, but she remembers that her grandpa was a good man and he gave people medicine for free and made Christmas tree ornaments out of wood in the shape of smiling Moons. And here she is again at the seaside, back at the starting point. The North and South Pole no longer exist. A mild south wind is blowing, and we stand on the pier surrounded by jagged, agitated rocks and the azure colour of water. Beneath the waves is the sand, which addresses the surface through them, changing the tone of the sea. As if she is the dry, light trunk of some tree, a trunk thirsty for water, we gently take grandma into our arms and raise her over our heads. Her head is now in the clouds she so easily forgets about. We stand motionless for some time and watch the sea. Our bodies, pillars for grandma's body.

Her body, you say, that's why we're on this planet.

Lined up beneath her surface like a little army, from oldest to youngest, except for a gap that yawns empty behind mother, and then the series begins again. Observed from the side, we look like a great spider that has perhaps lost just one leg. But it keeps moving. Towards the sea. Grandma doesn't notice that her son isn't there, she no longer calls her son to take her. Because now she's at the sea. Because she's at the sea. The sea that interrupts the story.

Lovers, Birds

When I remember when his face was between my legs, a face full of black hair, a face as detailed as a strand of hair, a soulful face that could have baptised people in the river Jordan; a face that loves femininity, and sometimes that's enough to create an entire little Earth. Independent. Self-satisfied. When I remember, I feel real. And I remember how the birds flew beneath the ground floor window, and their flight was pleasant not only to the eyes, but to the body — their flight was as if someone's hand was surely pulling them by invisible threads high into the air and then returning them to the Earth, but never all the way to the ground. They had to stop in the transitory treetops, far from the edge of the earth. And this is exactly how they flew then, and that's why they reminded me of that day in the days to come; because those birds always fly like that and then simply disappear, as if they were disappearing into the silence of the room, making the silence audible. He slept as I observed the birds and thought about how similar bicycles and humans are when they move at the same speed. The birds' flight permeated me; I think people like when the air is permeated with something that is about to disappear. The snow will melt, the birds will fly away, the petals will become fragrant and wilt. People like when the sky feeds the emptiness of the air. They like feeling warm, satisfied, like myself in bed with a body next to me whose details I am ashamed to look at because it's still unfamiliar to me, and might never become familiar to me. I'm afraid to face the details — I flee from them like birds from people. My gaze is constantly flying somewhere. It spins round in a circle, but actually goes nowhere. Immature and aimless like a chicken whose wings always fall back down to Earth. It was so lovely saying nothing in that bed, but despite that I began to talk, something about how his body's silence drank in the world around it, like a sea sponge drinking water. I imagined his whole body turning into water, because I so liked that he said nothing, and that when he did, he spoke French. I don't speak French, but I began talking anyways, because I'm not from the Far East, I can't keep quiet forever. Life is so short. It's nearly over. Just a bit more! Look! Life is just this afternoon. Little children are dying in this life. It seems to me that the Earth is going to explode. So I put him back between my legs, his face full of solid hair, a face as detailed as the curly hair on his arm, a soulful face that loves femininity, and sometimes that's enough to create an entire little Earth. Healthy. Indestructible. He, a tree. I, *earthwater*... But I told him to use protection in the end. You see, rubber protects me, but it pollutes the Earth... He, a tree on which white birds land for just a moment. Lovers, birds. To go into the birds, to dive into their flight, to borrow the shadows of their wings that flit about the walls of the room and disappear.

೧

Sunita (Soo-nee-tah) doesn't know how to write in Hindi, even though she does speak three languages. Only Sunita's mother's warm breath had conveyed the language of her ancestors to her. She never sees her language on paper because she doesn't live in India. She's never been to India. Just as it doesn't snow in her country of Suriname, her letters have never been stuck to paper. Writing and reading in Hindi seemed almost miraculous to her, just like the temperature falling to -20 in Suriname. Sunita only knows the Latin alphabet. Her mother's tongue is in her body, and it doesn't know anything about paper. Besides, paper flies just like language, just like birds, even though it seems sturdier. Sunita wants a baby so she can speak Hindi to it, a baby instead of paper. Paper is nothing but boring, mute material. Pieces of paper are also like fairies, like white spirits from another world. But not to Sunita. To her, pieces of paper are just bills, jobs to be done that get ripped up afterwards.

The baby will tell the rain "paanee barasna", and then greet it with "Ram Ram." Sunita is going to give this cold country a souvenir from Suriname. I have the feeling that her baby will be full of colour, as bright as the parrot she keeps shut in a cage in the bathroom. The bird constantly squawks, unsatisfied with its transformation into a living sculpture. Sometimes they let it out to fly about the flat a bit, and then the dark shadows of the wings of the white birds loom above her. Colourless, listless, but the parrot still bursts with green and red even though it's shut in, as if it has come from a distant galaxy to warm up the city! But it can't do anything from its cage, it can't do anything so long as the upper edge of its sky is a white ceiling. Let the parrot out to paint with its flight and its wings…! Surrender it to the white birds…! But they only surrender it to my shoulder instead, as I fear its small, precise beak (it will stop my flying glance as if playing darts) or it getting stuck in my hair. It flew into Sunita's hair on that day filled with the birds' flight, which all the coming days full of flight reminded me of. I came home, and flight was stuck in Sunita's hair! They seemed powerless, both the bird and Sunita, two powerless earthly beings whose nearness causes chaos. Then Sunita tells me, laughing, that Kishan, her "boy, not good," calls the parrot Sunita too. Sunita and Sunita, two small earthly beings. They used to have more birds in other cages in the house, and they were all called Sunita. They all pecked at Kishan's brain, just like Sunita. Sunita doesn't have a shrill voice — hers is deep and joyous, a voice like a frayed rope with string sticking out messily on all sides. She also has dark skin, but she looks more like a distant descendent of the Inca. Sunita too, just like the Sunitas, lived in a cage for a few years. When she came to this cold country, "Old Man" took care of her, only letting her leave the flat to go to work. He was the old man to whom the other cages belonged, which Kishan and Sunita would take care of occasionally. He had at least twenty cages full of birds in his house, and it's hard to believe that Sunita, the bird with the warmest smile, was there too. It's hard to believe that the old man shut birds from his country into cages just to remind him of his homeland. How could those caged birds even remotely remind him of his country, where they nest free in the bamboo, all blooming and dying at the same time? Or, regardless of the freedom of parrots, perhaps his country was actually entirely unfree if he had to bring it with him in cages to a cold country he still didn't love even after thirty years, a cold country in which only white birds are free...? He is also one of the Sunitas — they all came here in cages and remained in cages, because they had to eat. Here, the cages are a bit bigger — they can fool you. There is plenty of room to move about freely... The birds earn their own seeds. Sunita too, for years, brought seeds home for herself and the old man's birds. When she wanted to go to the theatre, the old man would tell her in Hindi — but I know Sunita in English — he would tell her: "Not go out. Out dangerous. You want to go to cinema? Here's the cinema!" He would go to the store and buy the largest television set possible and the best film possible and popcorn and give it all to Sunita so she could watch a film surrounded by the shrieks of birds. Likewise, when she wanted to go out to a restaurant for Indonesian food, the old man would run out the same instant and bring her all manner of culinary curiosities...! When he would come back, he would tell her in Hindi, which he also doesn't know how to read or write — but I know Sunita in her poor English — he would tell her: "Not go out. Out dangerous. Want to eat? Here eat!" And he would do the same for everything Sunita wanted, a princess in a golden cage. The old man did it all so she wouldn't end up in unfamiliar white sheets in the dark night, impatiently awaiting the birth of the flight of the white birds. The name Sunita translates to "well-raised." That's why Sunita made an agreement with Kishan, fifteen years her younger. She will be his caretaker in this cold country, and he will give her a baby. Because, "men not good," "this boy not good!" That's why Sunita wants just a baby but no man. When she was twelve, her mother chose a husband for her who cheated on her, and she had to cook for his entire family. So she decided: "This not for me," and went to a cold country to become a nurse. Tough girl Sunita now has her own flat and her own car — the only thing she's still missing is the baby she agreed upon with Kishan. Lovers, strange birds who sleep together while the parrot squawks in the bathroom.

Ying and Yang

Ying and Yang were next-door neighbours. Ying was still renting his house, even though he was over sixty, while Yang had long paid his off, even though he was only thirty-three. Ying had never wanted, let alone tried to buy the house, because the very act of renting represented a kind of freedom to him. It meant he could leave whenever he wanted, and that he didn't know where he would meet his death. Maybe his next house is only now being built... Or maybe a forest still stands in its place... Lovely — first the forest, then a building! An entire civilisational jump, an entire history of the human race in two steps. Things like that were still happening to him without his knowledge, and so he probably wouldn't be like Yang, he thought. Yang was only thirty-three, and he already knew where he was going to live and die! Oh, silly Yang, thought Ying. But he actually didn't bother too much with Yang. He was alright, that boy who sent satellites into space. A "cool" job, thought Ying slangily. To be above everything in the universe, only to spy slyly on the Earth! Hmph, a bit prosaic, but "cool," definitely "cool," as if it were important why the satellites were up there in the first place — all that mattered is that they were. Yang had explained that his mini-satellite was shaped like a square because it was easier to build that way, and Ying found this unusual. A square satellite, hmm... It immediately reminded him of a mausoleum, and so he didn't want to hear anything else about the satellite, the black coffin floating lonely around outer space. Brrrrr, it gave him chills. Was that really all...? No, that wasn't all. Yang explained that he was wrong — the satellite was alive! There is a special orbit called a *graveyard orbit*, and only in that limbo do satellites await their disappearance, which may or may not come... They continue orbiting on that trajectory 36,049km from Earth, an extra 321km above Earth's furthest active satellite... Ying truly pitied their cruel fate, the programmed fate of satellites let off the leash into the depths of space, but which still have to move along a given trajectory, which they navigate while they await their assigned death! They lose the ground beneath their feet, and they feel as if they are walking on asphalt, because even the air in space is inscribed with the word, with orders from Earth! Yang told him he was talking nonsense. What, did he want satellites and the Earth to wander around together in a drunken stupor? In that case, neither we nor anything else would exist. He smiled at him — he found the old man's naïveté charming. Ying only wrinkled his nose at his comment, saying that Yang couldn't understand anything further than the end of his nose, like some kind of programmed robot! But he wasn't truly angry. Instead, inspired, he went home to write an epitaph to the satellites, the human creations above everything human. They meet for coffee with the Earth, wrought by entirely different hands. They feel envy for its variety in their polished, empty surfaces — in their walls, which don't divide them from other walls, because the streets are so far away. As are the people at the windows. As are Ying and Yang, two neighbours who, regardless of the almighty providence of satellites, were about to get caught up in typical human problems. Oh yes, Ying liked satellites, but Yang didn't like his small, earthly dog! He couldn't stand him. He got the daily urge to punt him into space so that he could keep his satellites company, bark at them a bit, and finally leave him alone! Why was he always digging around in his yard? He had no business there! On the other hand, Ying couldn't stand anyone who didn't like his little dog, who went everywhere with him, on the tram and to lunch, all in the aim of helping Ying abandon his greatest vice — smoking. He decided to buy a dog so he could finally do something useful with his hands. To pet a lovely being, who certainly deserved it more than any filthy human! So he had to take the pup with him everywhere to prevent any potential cravings! Eventually, instead of cigarettes, he became addicted to the little animal! And woe to him who didn't like his little barking ball of fur. It happened one Sunday afternoon, when Yang callously kicked little Satellite (Ying had decided to name him this for a number of reasons: because the dog followed him like a little satellite, and because he had taken a liking to satellites thanks to his crazy neighbour) right before Ying's eyes. Ying was left speechless —a giant boulder fell out of his gaze and landed across Yang's entire body. He simply picked the dog up and went home, ending his walk. He tossed and turned all night, unable to think of the appropriate revenge. What he wanted to do was impossible: kick Yang's satellites so hard that they flew out of their orbit, that they disrupted the entire universe of satellites, that all satellites collided into each other, that chaos ensued and everything grew out of it again, some new universe that no one would ever dream had come about in such a banal way! Unfortunately, he didn't have such power, but he still wanted to at least hurl a pile of rocks into the sky! But even they wouldn't reach the satellite — instead they would simply return violently to him and cost him his head! He was absolutely powerless... And so he gave up on all that, and decided to stick to a tried-and-true method: he would put all his rocks in a row and build a wall. He would put his hated neighbour behind his property line, and neither he nor his dog would have to see him anymore! Within a few days, the wall had risen. A high wall that even surpassed the tops of their houses, because Ying didn't even want to see the chimney of that awful house — he could barely stomach the cloud that hung cold-bloodedly in the blue sky above it. Now the only place Ying and Yang could run into each other was on the street, and streets — thank God — only serve for leaving, so there were no serious problems there. Life continued peacefully. The dog could scratch at the wall to his heart's content — the insulation was extraordinary! However, after some time, seeing as life loves to take place outside of walls, the little dog somehow managed to wander into Yang's garden. As if the devil himself had lured him there! And Yang was apparently a man of rules, and couldn't handle those idiots who, even in the depths of space, crossed the trajectories of their satellites with his and collided! Don't people understand that crossed paths mean oblivion?! Boom, crash, all gone! Dead particles floating in space. He preferred those who spoke romantically about couples: "Their paths crossed, fate wove them together…!" What fools! And now, this bloody dog was coming onto his property again. He could never understand it! Why did one's property always have to border someone else's?! He wanted to be unhindered along his trajectory… So, this time, he singed little Satellite's little tail, and sent him home with a message around his neck:

> Dear Neighbour Ying,
> The presence of your dog in my garden is unacceptable. I have already explained a few times that I do not like dogs, because they are always wandering around somewhere. And however much they might dislike cats, they are very similar. So, this time, I have decided to resort to somewhat harsher methods and burn your dog's tail, much like street people do to cats. I am sorry, but I must teach you a lesson now to prevent it from happening again, and to prevent me from being forced to do something much worse.
> I wish you a pleasant day.
> Regards,
> Your Neighbour Yang

When Ying saw his puppy with his burned tail at his door, he burst into tears. He couldn't understand it — why did that man who sends satellites into space constantly get caught up in "worldly things"? Why, he himself, Ying, dealt more with his satellite than that idiot Yang! He broke down. He simply couldn't take anymore. Why couldn't his crazy neighbour leave him and his dog alone? What had they ever done to anyone? A little dog from Spain and an eccentric old pensioner? It came to him to call on God, to whom satellites represent nothing more than Earth's ground floor, and pray that he crush them all! He, no more than a poor old man, was powerless against the scourge of satellites. He didn't understand technology or GPS, nor could he turn it off! And yet his dog could be kicked as if it were no more than base garbage! His sadness and rage drove him mad. He cried all night and smoked twenty cigarettes for the first time in five years. He would have forgotten about the dog had it not whimpered all night along with him… In the morning, he sat at the table, read Yang's letter one more time, and wrote the following:

Dear Mr Yang,

After a tearful night, I will now answer your brusque letter, in which all your words are lined up in phalanxes; not a single word has broken rank — I shan't say — "as sprightly as a bird." Your letter, Mr Yang, shows that you are a cruel idiot who is missing out on all the life in between. Perhaps you've been spending too much time with your satellite, which has obviously spoiled you. It always goes wherever you tell it to, it answers every question you ask of it. Well, Mr Yang, that isn't life… So, for the very reason that I'm not a robot like you and your satellite, I won't pretend not to be hurt. For I am so hurt that I intend to cancel my lease and move somewhere else. I can no longer bear your presence in my life, not even behind a wall. Walls have holes, and not only people can walk through them — ghosts can as well. This is obviously no fairy tale. It's apparent that I can walk through walls, because I can't even bear your presence with a wall between us! Thank God I'm only renting this house, and am free to leave… I've always known I was smart for doing so! Had I been an idiot like you, the two of us would have had to suffer each other much longer, because it isn't easy to sell a house these days, as you know. And we would probably have fought about which of us would leave and which would stay. You should count yourself lucky I'm not a fool like you are, Mr Yang! Also, I'm not sure if you're aware of this fact, but there are organisms in the sea called tunicates. While they are still in their larval stage, they lead a free-floating life. They have a developed notochord (a skeleton), and they have a kind of nerve cord and a balance organ. When they find a suitable rock, they cement themselves in place. So, they pass from a nomadic lifestyle into a sedentary lifestyle, and at that moment, they begin a very interesting transformation! Because of the sedentary lifestyle they begin to lead, their bodies begin to simplify, making these organisms a brilliant example of devolution! Until they decide to settle, because of the presence of a notochord, they belong to the phylum of chordates, as does man. But adult, sedentary individuals lose their notochord, and so they can barely be considered chordates! Also, these intelligent "adults" digest their own nerve cord, which once controlled their movement, analogous to the human brain. It is often said that tunicates eat their own brain, because they no longer need it — they can then "zen out" in peace! I'm not sure if you've understood my metaphor, Mr Yang, in fact I'm sure you haven't, but I had to write it anyway. The homeless and the spineless can't live together, not even with the help of walls! This is the last time you'll hear from me. My dog and I won't be bothering you anymore.

Respectfully Yours,
Your Former Neighbour Ying

P.S. I wish you a great deal of success shooting your satellites into space, because that's all you know how to do. But still, I must tell you that I strongly hope that, one day, your system crashes and a satellite falls right on your head, you cold-blooded, sedentary shithead with nothing better to do than set people's dogs' tails on fire! You impotent moron!

Here is where the letter finally stopped. Ying was quite satisfied, tee hee! He had really shot his mouth off, even though that young, robotic monster wouldn't get any of it, nor would he be able to see his face when he read the letter. But he didn't give a hoot! The only thing that mattered was that he felt better. He walked over to his neighbour's front door and shoved the letter under it. Now all he had to do was pack, and in a few days he would no longer be anywhere near that revolting creature... But within a few days, in the part of the globe where Ying and Yang lived, a war broke out. Both Ying and Yang had known the situation was bad, but war hadn't even been in the back of their minds. Now wasn't the time for Ying to leave, unless he wanted to join the refugees, and it was still too early for that. Ying stayed in his rented house, and in place of a satellite, which he hoped would one day fall on Yang's head, a bomb fell on Yang's wall instead. But it wasn't only Yang's wall, it was Ying's wall too, as the wall had belonged to both of them. Yes — they actually shared what had divided them. Nothing else was destroyed except for the wall. The bomb had broken the barrier, and the houses again gazed lovingly at each other! Ying was as mad as a dog, and Yang was as mad as a dog. In perfect harmony, they barked at each other while satellites floated somewhere far above it all, and bombs fell about the Earth.

SwissCube

For as long as he could remember, Jean Yves spent more time than others gazing at the sky. He recalls his childhood as endless clouds and the squeals of children in the distance. He would lie alone on the grass, his face buried in the clouds, succumbing to the world of imagination. He tried to comprehend the world he knew, the grass on which he lay, in the white shapes of the clouds, creating a new universe according to his own screenplay. The clouds above him truly did exist, but within that existence, unlike any other phenomenon or thing in the world, they gave him the soft freedom to find something of his own within them. As if they had been created just for this purpose, to inspire people to create. He liked them… A combination of reality and imagination, tangible and intangible, a cursed border between worlds, and thus entirely elusive. They proved the truth of how worlds are momentary and passing, and how you can barely manage to build them or think them over before they vanish. No sooner would he see a car or a monster with a long trunk instead of an arm than the car would turn into a smouldering chair, and the monster would simply evanesce. Not once did he have enough time to design the infrastructure of an entire "cloud world". The monster would never sit on the puffing chair, the car would never drive across the crystal blue sky, honking merrily… He unconsciously learned that the world doesn't exist as a whole, and each small part of it represented a separate element to him. He was thankful whenever he was able to observe it so penetratingly and capture it, if even for a moment. Precious moments would then take the form of a cloud, a mere cloud, and he would always remember this afterward. When he would feel, he would always see the image of clouds before his eyes, not trying to be anything but clouds that want to go away and vanish, despite the fact that people try to see something else in them, "something lower," closer to their earthly world.

This meant that he neither wanted nor was able to exaggerate in the moments in which he did feel, to decorate them with stamps and vows. Words floated about his head just like clouds, and when he needed to say them, they would merely evaporate. As if the devil himself had swallowed them! He didn't feel they were meant to be uttered, because he was barely aware of them. He enjoyed them in a kind of half-sleep before he would even realize that he should have said some of them to someone. Deep down, he hoped they would end up stored on some invisible hard disk in his brain and that he would find them one day, even if only in twenty years, and say what he should have said to everyone dear to him, in defiance of the concepts of the present and the future, of space and time. Until then, until the moment when his soul might spit out the information, he decided to dedicate himself to his love of technology, and in addition to the clouds, to communicate with satellites, and potentially even aliens.

But safe trajectories sometimes go awry, struck by unforeseen life events… One of his first projects was the SwissCube "cube-sat," which was sent into space on the twenty-third of September, 2009, straight from India… On 18 February, 2011, when SwissCube first photographed the darkness of space, the three of us finally went out together for the first time. By the three of us, I mean Jean Yves, Anastasia, and myself. I had been Jean Yves' roommate for about a year, and Anastasia was a girl who had just landed in the West shortly before that. We met when she answered our advert to rent out a small room — which we called "the crate" — in our flat. In the end she didn't take the room, but the three of us ended up going out together anyway. It was a special night, because all the art galleries in town were open late. I remember Anastasia was excited because here, in this new world, she wouldn't run into anyone she knew. I didn't say anything, but I thought she would change her mind later; later she would miss the closeness of people and she would start seeing familiar faces in the faces of strangers. As I observed her face, happy and flushed because of everything new to her, she didn't notice me in the least. She stuck to Jean Yves and his satellite. In his terse vocabulary, Jean Yves explained how Swiss-Cube had photographed space for the first time today. Even though she knew absolutely nothing about satellites, she was taken by the fact that some tiny satellite, around seven hundred kilometres from Earth, just 10x10x10cm in size, had taken a picture of all of outer space this very day, even though the goal had been to record just one of its fleeting events — the aurora. This first photograph taken by SwissCube was almost entirely black, with only a bit of thermal noise in it. "The universe as a whole. Ever a *Black Square* on a black background..." said Anastasia, looking into the sky, certainly perceiving it as completely whole. I'm convinced that Jean Yves fell in love with her at that very moment, but he didn't say anything. Instead, just like in his childhood, he simply pointed his nose towards the sky. And so the two of them, unaware of their compatibility, looked upward in silence.

After that night out, nothing happened between them; Anastasia and I began seeing each other as friends. It was not only because of this, but because of Anastasia's passion for his satellite that Jean Yves withdrew even further into himself. As if his strong feelings had drowned the possibility of him uttering a word. He spent entire days working or observing the sky, which was turned orange by light reflected from the numerous greenhouses in the country. I would occasionally bring him news about Anastasia; I would tell him about how her life was developing and how she was managing, to which he would merely smile weakly, and nothing more. Once, I brought Anastasia over for dinner. She was a bit tipsy that day, and she was wearing a short, artificial turquoise fur coat that she refused to take off, even though it was warm in the flat. As we were laughing at something, the front door opened and Jean Yves walked into the room. I'll never forget his face when he saw her. There was no trace of jealousy in it at my having brought her home instead of him, no trace of anger — only calmness and nobility. It was then that I realized how strong and stable a man my friend truly was. Somehow, without words or touch, his gaze said with certainty that Anastasia's entire being belonged to him. In that moment of silence, as if what was happening around her had nothing whatsoever to do with her, she merely managed to ask: "And how is SwissCube, Jean Yves?" With a broad smile the likes of which I had never before seen on his face, he answered by simply nodding awkwardly and then excusing himself, as he had to work. This left Anastasia quite confused; her movements lost their unaffectedness, and she was taciturn the rest of the night, which looked even more tragic in contrast with her bright, turquoise coat. I was simultaneously angry at and inspired by the two beings beside me, and I decided it didn't make sense to call Anastasia so often anymore.

I didn't contact her for a while. The days passed just like before she had appeared in our lives, monotonously and without the liveliness of youth. In my life, I worked, I drank and talked, but it seemed as if everything could pass right by me without engendering even the faintest urge to hold on to any of it, whether a person, an event, or a story. I suppose this is what you might call life stuck in a rut, and that it's a normal occurrence,

never come. From somewhere in the back of her mind, the words of a melody she knew from a past life bubbled forth: *Loneliness of the world. Loneliness wherever you look. Fragments floating in the emptiness. The elements in the kitchen. Cupboards, cups and plates. The faint voice of the nightingale singing in the dusk of the night...* Jean Yves' excited voice shook her from her thoughts, in a tone she had never heard. "Here it is, it's coming, it'll be right above us soon! I hope we'll be able to establish communication!" Soon, Anastasia heard: "BEEP, BEEP, BEEP..." And again: "BEEP, BEEP, BEEP..." SwissCube had talked to them, and was informing them that its motherboard, its batteries, and its solar panels were all alive and well. Jean Yves's eyes glowed. Anastasia imagined the tiny object in space, created by human hands, that took exactly 98.5 minutes to spin around the Earth on its orbit. I'm sure that, at that moment, she decided to live in harmony with Earth's two satellites — the Moon and Swiss-Cube... She then heard "BEEP, BEEP, BEEP" once more, but weaker and weaker until it faded completely, until everything else on Earth was as it had been. The satellite seemed to have disappeared down the drain of outer space... But, in those three minutes, those three precious minutes, it was as if the two of them had become one, and even I along with them...

"That's that..." Jean Yves said curtly, and they slowly headed out of the building. On the empty field that spread before them, a girl was riding a horse. Anastasia would have been thrilled by the scene — a girl on a horse in front of the big satellite antenna on the building — had she not been angry at Jean Yves. "That's that," she repeated his words in her head, feeling as if he had just physically and mentally taken advantage of her. When he dropped her off, she just slammed the door of his car, and he slammed the door to his room even harder when he got home. I interpreted this as meaning that nothing had happened between them again, or rather that everything had happened.

I only saw Anastasia once after that. She told me she was leaving, because since SwissCube had entered her life, she couldn't stay in one place either. She felt like she had to go, and that her life would have no purpose on just one point on Earth — it was destined for a path instead. It seemed to her that the only real truth, the truth of life as it truly is, was that black satellite, alone in the black of space. The last thing she said to me before she left the café was: "We're all just a mass of lost satellites whose orbits are predetermined..."

Jean Yves, however, continued in his own fashion, at least until our paths parted ways. He was waiting for the day when, after twenty years, he would be able to tell people his thoughts and feelings. In one of our abrupt conversations, he told me how Anastasia sometimes contacts him from far corners of the globe, and how the only thing she asks is how SwissCube is doing, and never how he or I are doing. He usually, in one word, answers that SwissCube is fine. Once, however, he had to tell her with a heavy heart that SwissCube had almost died. They had to restart it, but luckily the Sun quickly filled its two batteries. It came back to life — and lives on.

THE PAIN MACHINE

That sunny morning, Hans didn't stretch his arms towards the sun, hidden behind the ceiling, as he had imagined the comfort of his awakening the night before. He had gone to sleep early enough, and he had been satisfied that his flat was tidy and all the work he needed to do was done. He fell asleep with the sweet smile of the righteous on his lips, the kind rarely seen on an adult. Yes, he certainly had worries too, but they didn't even evaporate at that moment — Hans simply forgot about them. His thoughts dallied a while on the convex border between sleep and wakefulness, and metamorphosed slowly into a dream in which they wore broad crinolines made of fog. Their contours faded, and they grew into pastel paintings. The man drifted off to sleep, looking forward to the sunny morning and starting his day with a glass of orange juice. Then he would go to the office, everything in order, just as it should be, exactly as he liked it... And sure enough, the next day was orange and the orange juice was sunny and Hans woke up on time without bags under his eyes... But, before he managed to stretch his arms out fully, he felt a horrible pain in his head. It spread from the top of his forehead all the way to the back side of his neck, as if he were wearing a cap of pain on his head... Aaaaaaaaaah, Hans screamed, but his scream went quiet and the pain continued on unchanged. He went to the bathroom and gulped aspirin, then went to the kitchen and drank a litre of tea and orange juice, convinced that he had come down with some sort of viral infection that would wane over the next few hours — if not by then, definitely by the next day. He set off to work decisively, but came back after two hours because the pain was unbearable. He locked himself down in bed and tried to sleep, but instead of sleep, the only thing that came to his eyes was undrinkable, salty water, the result of the horrendous pain. He went to the bathroom and took another ten or twenty pills, but to no avail. Not a single pill would help! After being unable to help himself, what else could he do — Hans called an ambulance for the first time in his life. The pain was so strong he couldn't even think, he couldn't even put together a thought like — my life is truly unpredictable, I never expected a day like this! He didn't even manage to consider where such a strong pain had come from. What could have caused it? All his thoughts had been dulled completely, like skipping stones sunken in the sea. The only thing that existed was hollow pain. The man with all the thoughts and daily obligations had disappeared. They decided to check him into the hospital, because when he finally arrived there, he was screaming in pain, screaming like a woman in labour. It was unbearable, it sounded like he was being skinned alive! All the patients in the hospital whispered to each other, they were all talking about the hollow screams that wouldn't stop, as constant as a highway to space and back. Each of them provided their own diagnosis for the screams. Some thought the man had been burned in a fire, others that someone had cut open his stomach, while others yet thought he was dying of unrequited love. The only thing no one had thought of was that Hans' head hurt. It seemed too boring a diagnosis… Maybe the patients would have stopped talking about this unusual newcomer had the doctors managed to stop his screaming. But not even the most modern pills and anaesthesia helped. The pain would always wake Hans up, as if he had experienced some kind of "superdeath," a death so painful that the pain brought him back to his screams, to life… and you can't be at peace, either in life or in death… Throughout the next fifteen days, the doctors did all the tests they could, but found nothing. Finally, as the cherry on top, they concluded that Hans was mad, and released him from the hospital. As they pushed him through the door in a wheelchair, his screams continued in the same intensity — no stronger, no weaker. He sounded like an air raid siren, its wailing warning the world unnecessarily in this case. And so, they unanimously decided Hans should be taken to an asylum, convinced that they wouldn't need to prepare a soundproofed room for his screams, as he would soon go quiet from exhaustion. To their great surprise, this didn't happen even after fifteen days. Hans, like the best hi-fi recording, kept on screaming aaaaaaaaaaaaaaaaa aaaaaaaaaaaaaaaaaaaaaaaa-aaaaaaaaa. He had turned into a pain machine. After they realised his screams wouldn't stop, the asylum no longer knew what to do with him. He was even driving the already crazy people crazy, and they decided to follow his example — they all screamed aaah, owww, or uaah, or they cried, or wailed, or whatever. The madhouse had turned into a real live madhouse! The madness could no longer be restrained. The patients drove the doctors so crazy that a few of them quit, because they simply couldn't bear such working conditions! Ninety per cent of the staff ran for their lives, while the small percentage that remained had to call various other institutions for help! It took five dozen people working together two days to get the situation under control. They moved Hans into a room that muffled sound, and Hans' aaaaaaaaaaaaaaaaaa, which seemed so unnecessary to the outside world, finally ceased to exist. The crazy folk mostly gave up on their own, while they stuffed the most persistent with pills. The madhouse finally went quiet, all sound disappeared, and it now seemed more like a graveyard. It was difficult to imagine the madness that had taken place there just a moment before. But Hans' aaaaaaaaaaaaaaaaaa, constant as a clock hanging on the wall of an empty house, continued. Experts began to find his case quite curious, and his situation slowly became what you might call a phenomenon — the fact that Hans hadn't died from exertion or hunger, because the doctors managed to give him just enough to keep him alive through IV or force-feeding. It was impossible for the man to keep screaming aaaaaaaaaaaaaaaa, healthily and decisively, as if he had just started the moment before! Didn't he need even a moment of sleep?! The experts gathered in his windowless chamber, armed with earplugs. He calmly sat on his bed, his back against the wall, and screamed aaaaaaaaaa, while outside the institution the sun was slowly setting in its own soft rhythm, as if it wanted to caress every inch of the sky, to slowly send the day off to sleep. The way Hans screamed aaaaa was much crueller than the way the Sun set, even though both actions continued day after day. Hans' way was located outside the world, outside the Sun and Moon, because he was in so much pain by now that he could no longer enjoy the tones. It hurt so much that he couldn't use his cries to produce even the slightest of melodies, the faintest of quivers or most powerful of sobs. The pain that he initially felt had somehow turned into his strength, his fuel, and Hans seemed to be simultaneously growing more painful and more powerful not only than the entire earthly world, but than the cosmos itself... Most experts weren't interested in this particular side of the Moon — they wanted to uncover the (physical) reason why this man still hadn't died, or at least given up. The news shook the whole world! Everyone rushed to Hans' little room! Black, white, red, and yellow, from countries both rich and poor, from war-torn lands and the rich western world alike — absolutely, positively everyone somehow managed to find the money for a plane ticket and fly on metal wings to see Hans! When they finally snuck into his room quietly (in contrast to him, who was so loudly screaming aaaaaaaaaa), they saw a man who was outside the world on the one hand, because they couldn't make contact with his pupils. On the other hand, every last one of them understood him, because his vocabulary was simple. Hmph! He was just repeating the first letter of the alphabet! Various experts, religious fanatics, and preachers watched him in awe; they observed the contrast between Hans' suffering face and the curt vowel "a" that emanated from his petrified, open mouth. The sound this mouth produced was firm and constant, almost unearthly, as if it didn't belong to some man named Hans, while Hans' face was white, as if all the floodwaters in the world were hiding behind it and desperately wanted to escape, but couldn't. A glance at Hans' face tugged at their hearts and filled them with sadness, while the aaaaaa Hans produced filled them with fear. Likely because his suffering face was something familiar to them, something they could sympathise with. The unbroken sound, however, was something no one had seen before, so they decided to shut it out with earplugs, and not only because of the volume. After doing this, research on Hans could finally begin. Soon, the experts took out their earplugs and scattered off each in their own direction, while a few of them remained to study the man in person. The departed experts gathered material about Hans' life, while those who had stayed behind studied every detail of his body. After a few days, those who left came back with tomes of paper with data on every last part of Hans' life. They didn't find anything especially interesting. Hans led a boring life, some might say, in which everything went off without a hitch! He was born in a prosperous country to prosperous parents, graduated with a degree in economics in the prescribed amount of time, after which he immediately succeeded in finding a job, where he sat at his desk and computer in his office from 8AM to 5PM, day in, day out. For some indeterminable reason, as the reasons behind such issues tend to be, Hans didn't have a girlfriend or a wife. Some of his friends even thought he was a homosexual, but the experts didn't really know how such unclear pieces of information might help them. They placed a question mark next to the field involving Hans' sex life, and decided to continue with the information they had, even though it wasn't of much help either. Hans was an average, well-standing man who put his back into his work by day, and followed local and international politics from his comfortable armchair by night. A war here, a terrorist attack nearby, a hurricane there, strikes here... After this, he would wash his dishes by hand (because, as one friend had stated — with the exception of television — Hans truly disliked technology, and so didn't even own a washing machine) because manual labour relaxed him. After finishing this job, he would go to bed satisfied. Hans was a laid-back guy, all his friends said, and they couldn't under-stand why he had been screaming aaaaaaaaa for twenty days now, this man who had never raised his voice in his life, let alone screamed without end! A peaceful man who lived for himself and bothered no one, nor did anyone bother him. This was more or less all the clever psychologists had managed to learn about this man! They brought all the paperwork to the hospital as fast they could, where the rest of the team was studying Hans' body from A to Z. Of course, these buffoons — whose brains lived in boxes whose thick membranes didn't allow them to visit other boxes and connect their own thoughts with other thoughts — discovered even less. Their conclusion was that everything was fine with Hans' body and brain. Why this man hadn't died yet and what was actually wrong with him was a complete mystery to them, and the game was already beginning to wear on them, as they didn't know how to play it. Everyone loves a game they know how to play and succeed at, otherwise they retreat to some other game! Most of the experts, after letting out a deep sigh of "ahh," went back to their own business. The only ones who heard this deep "ah" were the last two remaining enthusiasts, who were truly intrigued by Hans' problematic, difficult state. As opposed to the other experts — who had decided to study Hans as an object, nearly growing accustomed to his deeply sad face and using earplugs to block out his monstrous, machine-like aaaaaaaaa in the process — these two men had a bit more heart and brains. David was a molecular biologist, while Robert was a philosopher who, among other things, knew a great deal about religion and linguistics. The two of them, each in his own way, couldn't bear the narrow-minded approach of the other experts, and so they simply stayed quiet, waiting patiently for the others to get bored for want of finding a black and white answer and leave the room. When they finally did so with a loud "ahh" and slammed the door behind them, Robert began jumping as high as he could. David observed him with mistrust from the other end of the room. "Who's *this* guy?" he thought. "Probably some lunatic. Who else would end up last on the front lines besides me and a lunatic?"

"For god's sake, why are you jumping?" he asked red-faced Robert brusquely, but the sound of Hans' aaaaaaaaaa overpowered the question. Hans still hadn't budged. Like a sculpture screaming aaaaa, he peacefully sat in his place. This simultaneously saddened and fascinated David. But, according to his knowledge, problems were here to be solved, and however tragic they might be, it was necessary for them to simultaneously fascinate the researcher. True results have never been born out of uncreative boredom — only children! So the problem, now that it had appeared, needed to be solved in whatever way possible, and that was that!

"Hey, man, why are you bloody jumping?" he asked again after failing to receive an answer, and his forehead wrinkled slightly.

At that moment, Robert paused. His face was as red as if he had spent the entire day in the snow atop a high mountain. He looked at David calmly.

"What, do you think I'm some sort of madman who's going to keep jumping until tomorrow? Or better yet, that Hans' disease has infected me?! No, old chap, I certainly did mean to stop. But before I did, I had to use every last nerve to express my joy at the fact that my brain has slowly begun to unravel the knot of this caaaaaaaase," said Robert, arching his eyebrows and melting his aaaaa with Hans'.

"Oh really?!" said little David, taking an obstinate stance, his round belly bouncing happily. "Oh, yes, yes. So, enlighten me, what is it you've managed to find out…? I didn't see you running any tests, you were just sitting quietly in the corner the whole time!"

"Oh, tests! As if I believe in tests. What could they possibly say or prove to me? Tests are either 'yes' or 'no.' Anything else immeasurable can hardly be proven through tests," Robert answered contemptuously, and sighed. "But, fine," he continued more mildly. "What's done is done. Everyone believes what they believe, but I have a right to my own methods."

"And what might those be?" David had also eased off a bit.

"I simply think," said Robert with a sigh before turning his head towards Hans. David also went quiet. Both men observed Hans' suffering face, which seemed to have grown into a natural element before whose gaze all human beings felt equal.

"So… What have you come up with?" asked David carefully after a few minutes of silence.

"I've come up with aaaaaaaaaaaa! Let's get out of here and have a coffee, and I'll explain it to you!"

"What else exists in this case besides aaaaaaaaaaaa…? Maybe you could explain that to me, as well?!" David joked.

"What else exists in any case…?" Robert said, not budging.

And so the two men, hand in hand with Hans' suffering, left the soundproofed room. With his still steadfast aaaaaaaaa, Hans continued bringing the shell of his body and the shell of the room to life.

❧

When they went for coffee, Robert didn't reveal anything to David. Instead, he only turned his attention to what anyone who had seen Hans could have seen. Yes, it was the aaaa they could all understand, the aaaa that was the first cry of a child, the aaaa that was the first letter of the alphabet. We needed to start over, thought Robert. That man had been screaming aaaaaaaaaaaaa for nearly a month now, yelling one of the most universal things in the human world, and an entire team of experts was unable to figure out what was wrong with him... Isn't it a sort of paradox that even the first letter of the alphabet is still a complete mystery to people...? On the other hand, however, it was clear that the fact this was something "universal" meant that they might never discover Hans' secret... And this it truly wouldn't matter, finding a solution wouldn't be necessary, it could be forever left to contemplation were the issue not the pain of a man of flesh and blood. Therefore, they simply had to start from the scream, from universal pain. That way, thought Robert, they might reach a solution. Robert managed to convince David that they had to run tests on the simple thoughts that appeared in his brain in abstract form. He also admitted that contemplation wasn't enough on the issue of pain... He wanted to help that man, and it was clear to him that this would be impossible without a few tests. They should start from Hans' head, because that was where everything had started. They had to observe its every last detail — to, quite literally, split hairs. The tests David was to carry out would perfectly demonstrate the meaning of this phrase.

The two experts decided to go over Hans' head with a fine-toothed comb. "Trust in yourself and no one else" was their motto. Why trust anyone else? They got down to work and first carefully examined Hans' head from within, and when they didn't find anything, they began to examine it from without. A few days later, they still hadn't found anything. The tests claimed that nothing was wrong with Hans. So why had he been bloody screaming aaaaaaaa for a month now, the two newly minted friends asked themselves, scratching their heads. They should have been happy the man was apparently healthy, but how could they when he actually wasn't? They could only strongly, truly hope that they would find something unusual going on with Hans. And if Hans' hair hadn't suddenly gone entirely grey, not even the two enthusiasts would have come up with the unusual idea. The only thing they hadn't checked, something sufficiently lavish that had been right in front of their noses this entire time, something literally made for splitting hairs — was the hair on Hans' head! This time, David came up with the idea, and Robert teased him for not coming up with it sooner!

"It's because I don't split hairs by nature! Why pay attention to every single hair? Only psychopaths do that!" David was being a bit theatrical as always, but it didn't take him long to get down to work. He and his also theatrical potbelly, whose jiggling constantly drew attention to itself, strolled off to the laboratory, and they shut themselves in with various grey hairs they had plucked from Hans' head.

David and his young doctorate students began studying them, one hair at a time. His young colleagues thought he had lost his mind — why each hair?! He didn't debate them at all, partly because he shared their opinion. He would simply answer that they were lending credibility to the phrase "to split hairs." This answer left them speechless; all the nouns they had would fade in the shadow of this phrase, and they would simply continue doing what David had told them to do. In the silence of the laboratory, each expert held one of Hans' grey hairs in their hand, their different faces examining Hans' apparently completely identical hairs. When each of them finally delved into the unruly lines before them, and they all sat at a round table to compare results, they had plenty to discuss — the DNA of each individual hair was different. It didn't belong to the same man! Hans had an entire city of roughly two hundred thousand residents on his head, and this number was constantly growing — Hans' hair wasn't thinning, it was actually getting thicker every day! David nearly fainted at the results, and Robert certainly hadn't expected something like this either. Hans had become the unified scream of the entire globe. All those whose problems he had once observed while comfortably stretched out before his television had become an inseparable part of him. They grew out of his head, replacing thoughts he could no longer form because of the pain. After the initial shock, the two expert enthusiasts began to celebrate, and they grabbed one another by the shoulders and began to spin around in a circle. But the wave of happiness didn't last long, as they realised that Hans was still screaming aaaa, and the fact that they had made a big discovery didn't mean too much to them. They knew that a new, even more substantial wave of vultures was about to start circling around the poor man. It would no longer be just various groups of scientists — it would be the whole world, all those who could have potentially grown out of Hans' head! "Word" of Hans spread far and wide! Various people threw themselves at Hans' head, completely forgetting his tormented face. They began to stroke his hair or pull hairs as souvenirs. Some were even so egocentric that, despite the world being spread before them on Hans' head in an endlessly growing sea of hair, they searched for themselves (who knows on the basis of what, as all the hairs were apparently the same)! Animal lovers even showed up, who had somehow heard the (false) news that the feather of a murdered chicken, the hair of a monkey closed in a cage in a zoo, and even the transgenic DNA of a lab mouse had been found on Hans' head! An aggressive group of animal lovers physically attacked Hans' head, trying to destroy all the hairs that belonged to humans. Had the riot police not intervened, they would have killed the poor man! It's hard to believe the sort of mess the world around Hans turned into! So many hopeless people were turning Hans' case into an ever greater tourist attraction! The newspapers advertised his case as "A universe of pain on one head!" or "Hurry! Touch the pain of the world" or "Ordinary man from Western world is new Messiah!" They knew how to make money off of fools by stuffing them into planes and selling them grey hairs, and the fools — each for his own reason — rushed to see Hans or see themselves or see the entire world (depending on the individual)! It was a unique opportunity, and also one of the most popular slogans: "On Hans' head, the world, Hans, and you!" People no longer went to Bali or Cuba on holiday — they went to see Hans' head, to stroll across that tiny globe with their fingers… Political problems soon arose, as the government of the country where Hans lived wanted to ban visits to him. However, other states intervened, explaining that it could not be forbidden to visit Hans because he carried the DNA of the entire world in himself, and thus absolutely everyone has a right to him! His homeland still attempted to prove to the fevered world that this was an individual by the name of Hans, and not a dead world of international cells growing out of his scalp, but to no avail. The other states came together and called upon various laws, and Hans' country once again had to permit various tourists to come and see his head, looking for differences among the grey hairs! And yes, *those* problems also arose — Hans' head once again proved the superiority of the WHITE race! Why were all the hairs white, many asked themselves? On the one hand, the Ku Klux Klan rejoiced because Hans' head had finally provided firm proof that the white race was superior to all others. On the other hand, the church tried to soothe these rancorous statements with the logic that Hans' hair was proof that all people are the same, as all the hairs were the same colour. On yet another hand, some people of colour came who wanted to search Hans' head and pull their white hair from the world of Hans' head at any cost, as they didn't want to be there together with white people! All in all, it was the circus to end all circuses! Robert and David were desperate — they blamed themselves for what was happening to Hans. All the behaviour they had witnessed was highly illogical and unbecoming of adults, except for the church's statement. If you wanted to pull your hair from Hans' head so as not to be there with white people at any cost, then how doesn't living on the same planet with them bother you? And was the Ku Klux Klan not even capable of understanding the simplest fact in the world — that Hans had simply gone grey from stress? Didn't they understand that all races get white hairs? Oh, no no no — Robert and David clutched at their heads, unable to help Hans. That man felt the pain of the entire world, he was the most sensitive being in the world, and the world was tearing him apart mercilessly. And what was more — in all its rashness, the world wasn't just tearing him apart, it was tearing itself apart as well.

How many times must new versions of the same story repeat, Robert asked himself? How can people live so far outside the faces of others, outside of the world, and in doing so outside themselves? Where *is* the world, anyway?

As Robert withdrew into his thoughts, David was in the laboratory checking the hairs from Hans' face and body just to be sure. He didn't find anything unusual; all the other kinds of hair contained Hans' DNA. So, the face they saw was his alone, the body that sat stiff on the bed was his alone…

And the sound that Hans was making, thought Robert, was the sound of the whole world, the sound of pain and the sound of the first cry, the sound of war sirens and the sound of boats carrying food to distant lands. It was an "a" that wouldn't stop, one that represented a breath. *In the beginning was the Word, and the Word was with God, and the Word was God.* The emptiness of a breath around which a body formed…

But it was Hans' body itself that might be able to save him… David thought, chewing at a match. His body was entirely his, and his face was completely his, and his fingerprints were his, and those bloody vultures should leave him well alone!

In the blink of an eye, David materialised at the Foreign Ministry with the new findings and convinced a deputy minister to send a new document out. After a few days, they received an answer from HIA (the Hans International Agency).

The answer read that, according to the theories of leading experts, Hans was still alive thanks to the presence of the DNA of others in his hair, and so it would be impossible to isolate the man and prevent the entire world from visiting him. Without the DNA of others, which is likely activating in series, Mr Hans would be long dead. Unfortunately, his life now belonged to everyone. The only thing that could be done was to separate Hans' head from his body, but such a procedure would again impinge on human rights. Hans appeared completely healthy, and so this kind of euthanasia was out of the question. It was also unknown what would happen to the world on his head in that case. Were the hairs on his head connected with the lives of particular human beings who were currently walking the streets of some metropolis or not…? It was unlikely they would find out soon, and it was this fact that made Hans a danger to international security. He perhaps held the lives of thousands of people in his hands — strike that — on his head, and he could thus be considered a new kind of terrorist or a bio-weapon. For all of these reasons, HIA proclaimed Hans to be (potentially deadly) world heritage (because, in all reality, it could no longer be proven if Hans were still a human being, as his body was frozen and his vocal cords were constantly screaming aaaaa) that must remain under constant supervision. HIA could not completely forbid visits to Hans. People who satisfied HIA's conditions and asked for special permission would be allowed to visit Hans.

David couldn't believe his eyes when he read it! The tone was so cold it was as if they weren't talking about a human being who felt the pain of the entire world deep in his skin! Or perhaps, because of his excessive dose of empathy, Hans was no longer a human being…? Despite the anger he felt, David asked himself if Hans was still a man, or if the unbelievable pain he felt had taken him far away from humanity, closer to the world of machines? Hans no longer pained himself — the whole world pained him, and that was perhaps a somewhat different kind of pain, one no one had yet experienced. Weaker, stronger, who knows? Furthermore, David asked himself, how long can Hans even survive? When will he finally lose that voice, that used to belong to who knows who?! A voice of pain that turned into cutting metal… He thought and thought, until he finally came to a very simple solution of sorts. That's it — Hans would lose his voice when he and Robert hid him away from all those vultures! Whether they had HIA approval or not! There was nothing else that could be done.

Robert and David visited Hans together the next time. He was still, like the time before, sitting on the bed and yelling aaaaaaaaaa, as if he were truly begging to be euthanised. Before the two enthusiasts, a hairstylist had been to visit Hans. She had got permission to visit based on the statement that she wanted to give Hans a new hairstyle in order to show the world that he was a holistic place that could function only in structured, aesthetic systems. Only firmness makes a difference — pliant, messy hair is for molluscs, she claimed. When she finally reached Hans, she attacked his head with scissors, trying to commit a mass genocide and rip all of the hair out by the roots. The riot police had to intervene again, and albeit a bit lopsided, Hans' haircut was left in one piece — and the international mortality rate hadn't climbed either, HIA announced. The two enthusiasts sighed simultaneously in complete wordless understanding.

"You know..." Robert said, competing with Hans' aaaaa: "Do you know why I reacted to the 'ahs' of those experts who left? It was because I noticed that Hans wasn't screaming 'ah', but only aaaaa... As if something were missing. Interestingly enough, their 'ah' reminded me of the first letter of the Kabbalah alphabet, the *aleph-beta* — the letter *Aleph*. Aleph is pronounced 'ah', and it symbolises air, wind. 'Ah' is the first cry of a child after it's born... The word that existed in the beginning. *Aleph* is composed of three letters — Aleph, Lamed, and Peh. Aleph is breath, Lamed symbolises the head, and Peh symbolises the throat... This is how the strength of the wind enters your head, your throat, so you can pronounce *Aleph*, so you can begin to breathe and speak... Without air, we cannot speak and we soon die. But it seems that Hans' is the only case that counteracts this earthly rule. He says aaaaa, but it's as if he no longer breathes on this earth, as if he's missing that infamous 'h' to let him start breathing, or to — who knows — maybe lose his breath forever. Isn't that the only way for us to help him? The last chance before the world rips him to shreds completely? I can't stand listening to aaaaaa endlessly anymore — it doesn't fit in with our earthly world."

"I like the idea, old chap. I've also come to the conclusion that we must take decisive action! This situation has become untenable — some, like that hairstylist, come to see him out of purely fanatical beliefs, others complain that he makes them feel guilt for their easy life while half the world starves. Did you see it in the papers? Some woman stated that she could no longer live a normal life after discovering that Hans lives in her city! She begged city hall to try to take him to parts of the world where there was suffering and poverty because he would fit in better there, and then she could finally get on with more important things!" said David, shaking his head.

"Right. After all, reality is reality, and television is television... But sometimes, it's truly mind-boggling how heartless people can actually be. It seems so easy, as if you don't need some great deal of empathy or intelligence not to say such things or take such drastic hairstyling measures... But apparently that's not the case! The world is an Idiot!"

"And it's on Hans' head, ha ha ha!" David nearly died laughing, pointing at Hans' grey hair, which had become quite greasy in the meantime, as no one in their right mind had dared to touch it after HIA's various statements.

"Look how dirty and greasy the world is!" said Robert, pacing up and down in the cell, gesticulating almost gaily. His long body lent a refined nature to the cramped space...

"Terrible, yes... May they disappear in their filth... Now, tell me... Have you thought of a whole plan to help Hans? What have you come up with?" David asked, interested, as he played with the waves in his potbelly.

"Well, seeing as they no longer consider Hans a human being and they don't know what state he belongs to, since he's a true cosmopolitan, as it were… Aren't those reasons enough to launch that man off somewhere into the cosmos?!" said Robert mysteriously.

"Good lord — you mean into space?!"

"Yes, into space!"

"Aaaaaaaaa!" David croaked happily, finally creating a kind of melody with Hans' mechanical sound. "But how are we going to work that out…?" he asked, flushed in the face.

"I've got connections, don't you worry…" answered Robert, stroking his invisible moustache.

"Ha, ha, ha!" David began patting him on the back. "You're quite a piece of work! And, do you know what? I hope you're wrong! I hope Hans says 'ha ha ha' instead of 'aaaaaa(h)'!"

ↄ

And so Hans, the most cosmopolitan man in the world (who, among other things, they had stopped calling a man), very likely wound up somewhere far off in the cosmos. His body had vanished, and they could find neither hide nor haaaair of it. He most likely ended up on the Moon, as it's the nearest celestial body with no wind on it. Did Hans bring bre(aaaaaa)th to the moon, or did the Moon take it away from him? We shall never know. One day, back on Earth, no one noticed that roughly two hundred thousand people died in the same breath, but who knows whether it was because of Hans or if it was just a coincidence — a phenomenon that repeats day after day? Some still haven't noticed anything, while others who believe in conspiracy theories are searching for Hans here on Earth. The security of the world is at stake, you know.

The Dark Side of the Story

Every day, on the way to work, I would pass through a land full of empty strings hanging like laundry lines. My view from the train touched only these faint lines; they would occasionally struggle nervously with the wind, which seemed to be trying to arch them. Protected by the body of the train, I never felt the force of the wind on my face, but I knew that it had begun an attack on the lines, trying to give them something, or take something away from them — I couldn't say exactly what... In the end, it would always retreat, and they would remain hanging, victorious. Empty, horizontal lines whose existence seemed so unusual. Fields of thin lines — their horizons continued endlessly through the windows of the train, vanishing into the distance. I observed them every day anew with the hope I might understand something, find out where their beginnings and ends lay, or that someone might tell me they were rest stops for birds... Or that, if nothing else, someone would explain what it was about those taut lines that made me so uncomfortable, because nothing happened to them besides passing wind and invisible rain — even the birds always avoided them, drawn to the bare branches instead. Every day, on the way to work, I dreamt about how I would at least see the small, pink shirt of a child warming itself for a time in the sun, feeling its cotton melt beneath my fingers. Something to start with... But nothing changed. Every day, the lines simply hung empty. The story around me was so disturbing that the mere recollection of the feeling gives me chills, as if someone were twisting my spine or causing a stroke in a lab rat by probing it with a rod. A story that told me nothing and led nowhere, one in which there was nothing to hold onto, even though everything around me was hanging and the world was full of laundry lines that looked from the train as if they had been hung at a height human beings could reach. My train continued passing through the tense, empty lines of a musical score, but I was happy it was racing along at a hundred kilometres per hour, because that meant there was only another half hour left of the unease that put a lump in my throat and made my voice quiet and coarse. An unease that crumpled and crumpled my imagined pink shirt until it was no larger than my palm... Soon, though, I couldn't even bear that half hour. Instead, I rode with my eyes closed from start to finish, but unfortunately, the score had even spread to the space behind my eyelids, like the worst kind of metastasis. After some time, it seemed as if the lines had changed something in my brain, granted it a feeling of anxious resignation, like some kind of natural electroshock therapy, leaving a permanent line of a scar that lasted and lasted, ever-present, moving and standing still simultaneously. I observed human faces streaked with lines that time or sharp pain had written into their skin, and I was jealous that they could forget about those lines, as if they weren't there. Only mirrors could bring them back! Cuts in skin are also lines, lines that in some cases even bleed, so why didn't they care about those lines? Why didn't they work their way into their brains, throats, everywhere, like they did to me? What's the difference between those lines and the lines I saw before me? Their lines also endure, they are here with them, uncomfortably present even though no one needs them. Pure consequences, ones that also pressed at my throat. I couldn't explain it — it was as if nothing had been fully explained, as if it had all got stuck in the throat. Not a single thought was complete. The ball wasn't bouncing, it was simply rolling along the tarmac. Hands strolled about the landscape without bodies.

They no longer belonged to the left or right side, instead they only came together in prayer. That was all that was left. Only lines around me, within me, lines on which no one ever hung anything… And had I not taken the train to work once more, one day amongst all those paths of (un)stable routine, and had an older man not sat across from me, who knows how I would have managed to deal with it. It was then that someone spoke to me for the first time after a few months of riding the train, and I was no better; smarting from that world of lines, I sat silently and looked out the window every day — watching the lines.

"You look good, you young folk…" said the man, whose body had no head for me, because — as I have already mentioned — all creatures, things, and phenomena would get stuck in my throat, hidden and undigested, as if the entire world had been scrunched up into a lump.

His hands and his thin, chicken neck betrayed that he was an older man, although his voice, which was coming from a direction unknown to me, was clear and youthful. It seemed as if the open train window was talking to me… Was what he had said a sentence at all, or had I managed to relive only a part of it…? I don't know if he said anything else, but what I had heard didn't really appeal to me. A boring start to a conversation better left alone. I was thinking about only one thing.

"The lines," I said. "Do you see them? They emerge every day. Like worms on wet tarmac."

It didn't matter if I finished the sentence, because the only thing I spoke and thought about were the lines. As if what I thought within and what I said out loud had merged completely for the first time. Even if you cut off part of it, nothing would be missing, because it would still be a line.

"Ha, ha, ha!" the old man laughed, and there was nothing to cut out of his laugh, except for a few "ha's," which wouldn't have made much of a difference… His laugh filled me with anxiety, because I didn't know where it was coming from. It was quite uncomfortable — I was looking at his mute neck but hearing laughter, hearing that other world reaching out to me from somewhere, conquering my attention. As if the old man had passed from the physical into the metaphysical. From whose vocal cords was the voice coming?

"Lines… Hmmm. Yes," he repeated seriously. "Have you never heard of a story that couldn't be written because the writer didn't possess all the knowledge in the world he needed to truly write it as it should have been written? Do you understand that no one in the world can succeed at this, and that it will never be possible…?"

A question mark at the end, I thought. The sentence must not have been cut off, because the question was fully put.

"Can you explain, please?" I insisted he repeat what he had explained.

"All the stories in the world, at least the ones we know of, have been partially created through ignorance. A true story, the 'story of stories', doesn't exist, because no writer has ever possessed all the knowledge necessary to select the right knowledge for the story. Every writer, unfortunately, chooses one line, makes his move from the vantage point in which he happens to find himself, forgetting about the 'Dark Side of the Story.' You know, just like with the Moon… The dark side of the story…" He grinned. "Every story has its dark, hidden side, which we will never see!" he continued after a brief pause. "It isn't the shadowy side of what we've written — for example — but rather of what we actually should have written within the space of the story, but didn't. So, all in all, every story ever written is a lie!" the old man spoke out of some faraway throat, perhaps from some distant black hole, while his grey suit fell in regular folds to the floor of the train across his two neatly crossed knees.

"A lie…?" I repeated, stunned. "Isn't that the point? Aren't stories supposed to be false? Works of imagination…? And if we ever do attain absolute knowledge, who knows if we'll even have the need to write stories afterward…" I said quietly in the empty compartment, just now noticing that it was full of empty chairs. The train left line after line behind us, but new ones kept appearing.

"What if, what if… I don't want to get into that… But I can't possibly agree with your first claim!" exclaimed the headless old man, slamming his palm on the small table in the compartment. His shoes drew my attention — made of worn out, brown leather, they almost seemed to be poking fun at his formal suit, which certainly didn't have a sense of humour. The kind of shoes worn by the kind of worn-out old men who play the accordion for change on the street…

"You're wrong…" he repeated decisively. "It's through knowledge that stories are supposed to reveal truths, which have nothing to do with knowledge in the end. No story has ever been written that is simultaneously true and invented. A story that is true because it knows all the paths and possibilities, and chooses the right line, the one to stick to, the one to bloom on, and — even more importantly — chooses how it will bloom… Do you understand? It's not all that complicated."

I didn't reply to his comment. I realised I could now be sure that it was his last word, even though I wanted more. But nothing had been cut off. Nothing had been missed. I finally felt better able to cope with the lines.

"But the lines! The lines!" I yelled, jamming my finger into the train window. Why am I repeating myself when there is nothing to cut off? I asked myself.

"Aren't the lines around you the truest story you've ever seen? There's nothing to single out. There's nothing to point at. And the background is the grass. And the sky," the headless old man pronounced calmly, the top of his neck as smooth and rounded as the finest pebble on the beach.

"I wasn't looking at it like that... I thought they didn't lead anywhere," I returned, thoughtfully. At that moment, the lines looked as pliable and blue as the sea... And the world seemed full of possibilities. After just a few moments, I excitedly began to swallow words, asking questions:

"Do these lines represent the story of writers who chose one path without knowing of any others?

"Do the laundry lines hang so that we can hang up anything we want on them, even things that don't hang?

"How is the story read? Depth-wise or from the train?

"Are the lines thin proteins of hair, a DNA screenplay that needs to be read, or are the words hidden between the lines?

"Is this story a passenger on all the trains in the world?

"Oh, is a bare tree its closest relative in truth, as it has taken root justly and spread throughout the world, and lets some bloom while letting others wilt?

"What happens when you sneak under the laundry lines? Why are all the lines in the story the same?

"And wait, it seems like the train sometimes crosses the lines, is it not constantly parallel with them?!"

"No, you wait!" the old man interrupted. "Stop! This is important!" he croaked, but the train just kept going at full tilt. At that moment, I imagined him running after the train we were on. My head was stuck out the window and I was waving to him as his elderly legs galloped along the tarmac, his long trouser legs dragging through puddles of rain.

After coming back to reality, I asked him a bit coldly: "Why did you interrupt me? I thought the answer lay in numerous questions that can't be cut apart, questions that are like spores for entirely new stories. I thought that was the only true story — a whole story made of question marks that continue endlessly… Because that kind of a story is teeming with life. We live so long as we ask questions."

"You're right," said the old man calmly, turning his non-existent head towards the window while his neck remained motionless as a statue. "I won't say anything more…"

"Come on, tell me, man! Now, please! And please, for god's sake, stop whistling!" I told him angrily, but the sound of whistling grew louder and louder. The melody reminded me of a march, or something like one.

"Well, fine…" He stood, the words interrupting his whistling. "I interrupted you because that's what you said was important for a 'true story.' Your remark about questions is correct. I share your opinion. But some things have already been cut off, while we must ponder over others. Out of your cornucopia of questions, I recognised just one that is important to the story. You must ask many questions before you find the right one. You'll get better at it in time, I'm sure of it."

That nasty old man turned his non-existent head away again, but this time in silence, without whistling. All the sound in the compartment died for a moment. I was so curious and impatient that I nearly forgot that those hurtful lines even existed. Strangely enough, when I closed my eyes for a moment, I could no longer see them stretching before me into the distance. Instead, I saw the old man's face. He had piercing, blue eyes. Two slits with blue eyes in them. And wrinkles that drew circles of various sizes across his cheeks. And thin, dry lips, like all old people…

"But, is it true that the train sometimes crosses the lines, it doesn't always run parallel to them?!" I was persistent, and I nearly sang out the question. I began to shake the old man by his shoulders, and since his neck continued on to his head in my thoughts, I applied the same principle unconsciously to the rest of the parts of his body, like his shoulders, for example — parts that don't continue on to anything in accordance with long-accepted rules... But still — I don't know why — a lock of blond, female hair, like the skin of John the Baptist, fell across the old man's shoulders.

"You're repeating yourself, miss — you see that you're repeating yourself. Ha, ha, it makes sense, after all, doesn't it...?" The old man nearly died laughing.

"But the answers? Do they make sense? Come on, please, tell me the answer..." I asked impatiently.

"I don't have anything to say besides what I've already said. The train truly does cross the lines sometimes.

"Try and imagine what it would look like if the train only ran parallel to the lines. In that case, it would always miss them or it would always meet them... Whole and equal, they would follow it the whole time like another set of tracks...

———————————————

———————————————

"You would never have the need to stop, to cut the broken threads, would you? It would be a kind of unification of time and space. The traveller would sit reading in the train forever.

"On the other hand, now imagine that you're surrounded by various vertical lines... You would have the feeling that you've missed too much. The train would cut every colour, every detail, every fleeting touch into tiny pieces, and your gaze wouldn't have time to stop on any of it.

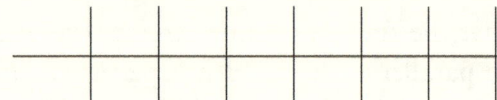

"That's why the train has to cross the lines sometimes, or at least that's how I see it. Just by allowing itself to cut their endlessness, it creates a new source. A beginning that is also the end of the line. The story did begin, but not with a stroke from a single point in space, but with the cutting of a line in a spontaneously chosen place. It began, then, with its own end."

"Is that what we call 'freedom,' in other words?" I asked the old man as I calmly looked out the window, and it seemed that the only thing I saw or could see was the view through the window, which somehow always found itself between the lines... Maybe the old man's voice really was coming from that throat...?

"Freedom?" repeated an old lady quizzically, her hair likely dyed blond. The words emanated from her oral cavity. She wore a spring dress with no body. I imagined the entire old man in his grey suit beside her. They were dying. Together.

A Mortal Story of Immortality

When I was still fairly young, I remember my father would tell me about spirits. I would lie in my little bed, and he would pat my cheek, telling me words before sleep. I remember he would sit, and he seemed static and thoughtful compared to my scattered, carefree toes under the covers. The room was warm, the air would become visible, and my father would spin yarns about spirits even warmer than the room, spirits who weren't icy — spirits drenched in kindness. He would recall how they embraced, he and my late mother. He whispered in my ear…"Son, you'll never be afraid of ghosts, because you'll know they're as warm as summer, and that they repeat themselves eternally like summer, ever thirsty…" he said, thinking of hugs. He also whispered to me: "Hugs are one of the rare shared things in the world. Look, see how silly it is when I hug myself? I look like I've tied myself up!" Laughing, he began to tighten his fingers around his own neck, pretending to be running out of air. At that point I jumped on him, trying to save him from his own hands, and we tickled each other, laughed and wrestled. His arms, of course, embraced me in the end, and mine then wrapped around his shoulders. "You see…" he said, panting. "Our interwoven arms here are a spirit, the single great spirit of all our ancestors. What do you think? Where does all that love go that has come about between people since time immemorial? What do you think happens to it?! It enters us, only to go somewhere else, already in our spirit-hands…" I certainly yawned at that point, and he surely said, like he had many other nights: "It's time for bed now! Let me kiss those little, thirsty spirits!" He then kissed my hands and left the room so quietly that it seemed as if he had passed through the walls. I observed my hands in awe for a time, wondering if they really were spirits (or if the spirit was just my silly father!), and if I really could talk with them. So I addressed the both of them (because father had said that only together did the two of them make a "halfhug") and waited for them to answer. They were ghostly white in the warm dark of the room, as if the Moonlight itself had been reincarnated in their palms, leaving only the pipe-like space of our fingers to our beloved ancestors... And while father slept soundly in his bed, convinced that his son would never be afraid of spirits, I tried to bury my own hands under the covers because they gave me the chills! It seemed as if they were a different colour and scent than the rest of my body. I did everything to keep them from escaping out of the subterranean world of the covers into the world of the living! This unusual game truly lasted three bloody hours before I finally drifted off to sleep. In the morning, thank God, they seemed warm and tame again, like the milk father brought me in bed...

"Father on my bed" is the first "picture" I remember, and even in this picture, he is already obsessed with death. This, one of my generally rare memories of my father, is etched into my brain in the form of a picture, because his obsession with death would take him far from pictures. In the coming years, I wouldn't have the opportunity for calm, static pictures of memories (except for the pile of pictures of him which I would just as obsessively produce with my camera), because my father was to discover a very simple, magical formula for immortality. Not out of selfish reasons, but not to leave me alone! For I had no grandmothers or grandfathers, nor aunts nor uncles — just one silly father. Silly, but still sufficiently sane that he did his best to hide the fact that, as the world would say, he had lost his marbles! This is why he organised his life such that he had as few friends as possible (read: enemies that might spy on him!), and such that he stayed within his own four walls as often as possible, hidden from the world. He forbade me from bringing friends over, or even from having friends at all, because the more people were around us, the greater the chance they would take my father away from me forever! And so, in time, the son also became a lunatic like his father. We grew into an unusual relationship, one perhaps appropriate for foetuses and wombs, and not fathers and sons, separated by an umbilical cord since the very beginning. Somewhere in my hindbrain, this all became clear to me quite quickly, and so it has remained until this very day... Oh, how many times I've longed for the mother I never met, convinced that everything would have been different had she survived! I wouldn't need immortality at all, then.

It all started when I was nine. Three years after the story of the spirits, my father sat me down officially and announced that he had discovered the formula for immortality, or rather, that he had simply decided to apply what many others had already discovered. He said that he had been searching for the answer intensively since my mother's death, because he didn't want me to ever be left alone in the world. Our life was about to change, and we would have to adjust. One day, if I wanted to, I could also use the immortality formula on myself, but I was too young for now. He told me to try and memorise every line of his face, because I wouldn't really be able to see him this clearly anymore. This would be the last time I saw him in his "standing phase", "statically imbalanced" like this, he thundered decisively, and I drunk in the tangible picture before me as if there were a spirit before me, or as if my father had just announced he was leaving to the next world. I was terribly afraid — I haven't experienced such great fear since! I dashed into my father's arms, and he hugged me tight. Within his embrace, I asked him — aren't spirit-embraces always static? What will become of them now…? He told me not to worry about a thing, that everything would be fine, because he wasn't going anywhere. The two of us would be together for a long, long time to come. But to achieve great things in life — and even little ones — great sacrifices are always necessary. Tearful and frightened, I fell asleep in his arms, and when I woke up in the morning, he was no longer beside me. I went to the kitchen, and there I found him, bouncing quickly on the balls of his feet, almost hopping from leg to leg, eating pork cracklings off a plate. At first, I was happy my father was so cool, and laughing like a silly, playful animal, I began bouncing ecstatically along with him. "That's it, boy. The whole philosophy of (im)mortality is hidden within motion itself. I have to move as fast as possible forever, flow like a waterfall, spin like the Earth, to become immortal. It's very simple, but no one has tried it yet, at least as far as I know… I assume no one has been brave enough — they've been convinced they would break their bones, collapse, or who knows what else… Also, it wasn't even possible before the invention of the wheel, because human beings in constant motion still have to sleep, don't they? I know you're about to say that the Earth is also constantly moving, and none of us are immortal, but the Earth's movement is so fast we don't even feel it. My theory is that I have to feel motion constantly in order to become immortal! So, from now on, I'll have to sleep on night trains, which means you'll be alone at home at night. But we don't believe in frozen spirits, so it won't be a problem, will it?" he said, taking me by the hand and pulling me into the heights, up towards the ceiling and on towards the sky. I accepted these words of his, even though I hadn't understood anything, just as I didn't understand what I learned about motion shortly thereafter in school. Just like how others had got used to fathers who wore suits and ties and carried briefcases, in the blink of an eye, I got used to the fact that I had a father who moved constantly in order to attain immortality (and who was still a bit sceptical of the success of his mission, because he wasn't sure if he'd started moving ceaselessly in time — he thought the ideal age to begin was twenty-five, the age when we stop growing, when the body stops moving upwards). When you think about it, there wasn't much of a difference between these two opposing types... My father was also able to feed me, however he had to now work exclusively from home so people wouldn't see him moving constantly and put him in the looney bin with a diagnosis of "eternal motion." And, crazy as he was, he would have surely told them (as he told me day after day) that the Earth was constantly moving as well, and in that case, we're all a result of its madness, and that without (that) madness, we wouldn't even be here! Hee, hee — I would often imagine that situation, and regardless of how much that crazy father of mine wore at my nerves in time, I always enjoyed the thought. As if it kept me from falling off the path of normalcy! And so we — but my father especially — eventually settled into that eternally imposed movement. The whirlpool we had been sucked into had no more nuances or differences. It was all one, great, monotone TICK-TOCK — although if we hold to my father's theory, time wasn't passing for him. His physical state, you see, had become more "fluid" than "still". Through endless motion, just like the flow of a waterfall, he had persuaded his own stiff carapace and every iota of his body that was not made of water into believing they were also one of the molecules in a waterfall, and that he was one hundred percent water — pure, transparent time. And time, although it constantly vibrates and flows, is solid and insensitive to anything, and my father eventually became similar to it. Because all the traces time leaves on us throughout our lives, all those wrinkles on our face, are only the scratches left on us by time's fingers — fingers that never manage to catch us, because we always slip between them like fish, sensitive to everything it is not. I often feel we are the product of its flow, of its beautiful vibrations, which have little to do with that dominant melody of empty sky.

In the first years of my father's motion, I was still able to talk to him — at least in small doses — although he had already become a ghost of the man who had once told me ghost stories on my childhood bed. At the beginning of his search for eternal life, he even seemed to want to talk, but I was the one who would get annoyed at the first sentence, because I would run out of patience for a conversation wrapped in eternal non-stillness. Wasn't it enough to move with words?! That's why, when I was in an exceptionally good mood, I would try to take him out for a walk — because it was the only way to feel as if I were talking to a normal person. It was impossible to talk to him at home, especially because he wasn't the constant Earth, which practiced only one kind of movement. He was just a man, apparently not up to the task of eternal motion, and he would constantly change his mode of expression! How intolerable it was! He would hop for a bit, bounce on one leg a bit and then on the other, spin around in a circle like a dog for a while, rotate around his own axis (to contemplate)! Oh, how many times I tried to convince him to stop, laying out the example of the Earth, which is moving and yet still to us — a feat he would never achieve because he was a man, a little, stupid man! I tried to convince him that the Earth suffers silently so that we might live on it in peace, sometimes stopping, sometimes moving, and — unlike her — talking! This idea of his was disturbing the natural cycle completely! Soon, he even became annoyed with me, happily commenting that immortality also disturbed the natural cycle, and that my "anti-reasoning" only made his head spin! These were the last gasps of our communication, because my father soon passed into a different state. Finally, I too gave up on anger, trying to convince him to move his hands and head, to give his legs a break, to not be such a slave to his own self-imposed rules! But he didn't hear me. He truly never heard me again. He only moved and ate, moved and ate, moved and ate... My father, a new, unusual species of organism... Once, I even tackled him to the floor, squeezing him tight in my arms, but when I let him go, he wordlessly stood and began moving again. He no longer needed the help of night trains, either, because his state of trance required no sleep. And so I gave up on violent, physical measures, and began photographing him madly in order to stop him. Paradoxically, photographs seemed to bring back his peace, his life, and his spirit. When I observed them, they didn't awaken any nostalgia in me, like in other people, nor did they bring back long-past, now unreal moments. No, for me, they engendered a feeling of reality and faith in the future. Faith that reality can be like it is in a photograph. It's unbelievable, but my father was only real to me in photographs. I could talk with him in peace. I could observe him in peace. I could be afraid for him. He was like all other fathers... His constant spinning was already making me dizzy, and even I slowly began to believe that he would never die. My camera brought me back to reality, and it was the only reality I could share the truth with. I couldn't tell any other human beings — at first my peers at school, then my colleagues at work — that my father had been hopping all day, every day for years, and that he had spent his nights lolling about buses and trains with alcoholics and drunk college students. I couldn't tell my colleagues: "You know, he's one of those bums you know from the street at night." Not because I was embarrassed, but because I know that there's still a chance the old man's right! I almost believe it even today. Who am I to disturb his life's work, or maybe the greatest discovery in the world? I'm just his son, who will neither become immortal nor have a life. A son who would have only a crazy father in his life, or perhaps a genius father? The fact is that the old man is ninety years old already. He's in exceptionally good shape, better than me, because he's still constantly moving, and what ninety-year-old can do that? His face barely has any wrinkles. Sometimes it seems to me that wrinkles appear and disappear as if on the surface of the water, all of which confirms the theory that my old man has become pure, transparent time. His body is still here, although it's so thin you can barely see him when he moves. He hasn't spoken in years; he forgot language long ago. If he did try to speak, his speech would probably be unintelligible, sped up like when you press 'fast forward' on the VCR while a film is playing... Strangely, from the moment my father decided to become immortal for my sake, every sound he uttered, every motion he made, every kilometre he passed in every way and in every direction placed him further and further from me. Unafraid of losing my father, I lost him first of everyone. And when many of my friends lost their fathers or mothers, I was jealous of them — I wished my father would finally stop forever so I could finally feel him, so his complete disappearance from this Earth would allow me both loss and gain... Only then would I finally be born, the little son of a great father. Like this, I had never had him, nor had I truly had anyone else because of him (at least so far). The only person I was close to had become a spirit living in between life and death, one that would never choose either of the two. He would just keep on hopping! Even now, as I write this, that madman is hopping, hopping, hopping, hopping endlessly...! These words will pass, I too will soon pass, the end of the Earth will come to pass, but that old loon will be somewhere in space, somewhere cut out of everything that exists, still hopping, and maybe some new world will be born of him. I think it's possible, but I'll never find out, because in that case, my old man will outlive me! He'll outlive us all, because I hope there won't be so many people crazy enough to give up on life and embraces in the name of love. To become a different kind of spirit than the ones they believed in... On the other hand, maybe the old devil will stop moving in the end, for the Earth itself surely will, and the word 'motion' along with it — and perhaps this itself is proof of the inevitable end of absolutely everything and everyone.[2]

---

2   The Croatian original of the final sentence of this story contains an untranslatable play-on-words involving the word "disappearance" (*nestajanje*), which is then divided to change its meaning (*ne stajanje*, "not stopping"). A literal translation of the final sentence would read as follows: *On the other hand, maybe the old devil will finally disappear, just like the Earth itself, because in the beginning was the word, and the very word "disappearance" [nestajanje] consists of "not stopping" [ne stajanje] — and perhaps this itself is proof of the inevitable end of absolutely everything and everyone.*

A Story Written in Sound

Silence was on paper before the word would ever be written. 'S' beat softly within her, like a chick breaking out of a white shell, emptying what was once whole. That is how it is with the silence behind words, with the soundless gesticulation of hands that form something out of nothing more than air. She was somewhere in the fibres of the paper, crumpled and thin, she hid in the flatness, balancing along a border that could give rise to both convexity and concaveness, but must not do so at any cost. Then someone came along, because someone always comes along, and crumpled the paper... It was her last breath — in this case, a cramp. Silence dies painfully, she is always heard, even when she whispers — her whisper is incisive. People are much quieter when they die, as they move on to wordlessness, but for silence, words mean death. "In the beginning, there was the word", a speech was held at silence's funeral... The universe, water, a mouth — these are the sanctuaries silence created for herself... But people sent rockets into space and they sent submarines under the water, and they began saying terrible things to one another, and she moved further and further off the closer they came to her, and it didn't even dawn on them that the universe is constantly expanding because of the noise they were making. If they quieted down, if they shut up, maybe the universe would begin to shrink. It would get smaller and smaller, until in the end, it would be nothing more than a single, solitary word, the word "word", which would echo silence, because it is the word of silence, while the word "silence" is much too dazzling a word. Then everything would start over, because that's how it has been and that's how it will be… Silence is always running from words, and yet she is so alone. Always unsatisfied and restless. Sisyphus' closest friend, who loves being swept away by the beating of birds' wings. She finds it such a comfortable, ecstatic death… There is only one other death she loves to die besides this one, and that is the breath of the slumbering, because between their inward and outward breath, there is a moment when she is reborn, a tiny, nested moment like those little holes between a woman's collarbones… She isn't so fond of other deaths, and there are truly countless ways for silence to die. She can burn up along with the wood in the hearth, she can evaporate while the cat drinks its milk, and she can be picked along with a flower…! Has anyone ever counted all the sounds in the world, and all those melodies that come about that represent a kind of purgatory for silence? She's neither in heaven nor on Earth, and music is the moment in which silence comes to an understanding with man, the moment when Silence is like man, and man is like Silence. They are related, those two — there aren't many phenomena or creatures in the world that can disappear in as many, various ways as can man and silence. Water only evaporates, fire can be put out in a few ways, animals never commit suicide. Plants die in near silence, just as they lived in silence; that is why silence loves them, alive and natural within her. Other living creatures always have to restrain themselves from making a sound in order to finally hear their ears' own ringing speech. And so silence much prefers automobiles full of powerful motors to weak people, who are constantly rustling around in her. Automobiles roar through her like a meteor and tear her in two, while people maim her as they open windows and doors and as their shoes ring out on the hard pavement. Silence is truly damned, because as soon as she wants someone, she no longer wants someone, because as soon as she gets the urge to express herself, she vanishes. So, similar to man once again, she often settles with him in new places on Earth. Alongside him, she lives parasitically in the womb, and there in the windowless silence, the two of them truly laugh, while the endless, soundless soles of human feet sprout on the grey, sandy coast.

The Ground

At first, the ground of the Earth was level and flattened. Breath barely fit in it; it merely smouldered, wrenched within the thin strands of its body. The Earth was a straight line, although nothing more than a round path within the universe. It spread across the world endlessly, all the way to where a few horizons met. No one and nothing disturbed it on that path — the path was its alone, and everything alone was the path. Completely polished, without holes or indentations, it merely reflected the Sun, and the sun reflects by moving ever closer to you, into your throat and your bones, your mind and your thoughts; its reflection sinks into your body. Rays of sun, pieces of crumbling boulders, broke invisibly yet heavily against the flawlessly smooth surface. The line almost shimmered; it was so stalwart and unbroken, so uncompromised. It was almost the unified reflection of all potential, uncreated reflections. The ground stretched on, raced towards itself to unseen lands. The camera recorded it from above as it went further and further, and all was ever the same. Only the camera's moving glances proved that something was changing, that the place was some other place. The ground thought: "Of course everything on me is the same, that's why I'm called by one name. Otherwise I would have more than a hundred names. This way, I'm simply "the Ground", and that's all there is to it." So it continued along the same path, in all directions simultaneously. The story might have ended here meditatively. However, a whole host of strange circumstances unfolded that the Ground couldn't absorb, and had it had a head, it certainly wouldn't have remained level.

All at once, plants began to grow in the ground, animals began to run across it, and with their tiny feet, people began to stand on it. All these minuscule creations were walking on the Ground or standing in it, but the Ground neither understood what they were, nor why it wasn't one of them. It wanted to communicate with them, but its breath got caught in the stems and trunks of various plants. A thought could barely cross its mind without some new tree sprouting out of one of its pores! Roots branched through the polished plain of the ground, aggressively piercing their way out, and however much pain the Ground might have felt, it still found the feeling pleasant. And the most pleasant — just to its liking — was the sprouting of flowers. It was like true acupuncture! But not a moment had passed before animals began to run on it and people began to walk on it, and the Ground could no longer concentrate from being unexpectedly bombarded with exclusively living information! So much was happening to the Ground, it was living so much life, and yet it couldn't catch anything, grasp anything, comprehend anything. Just imagine that endless shock, the unceasing motion that was happening to the Ground and to all of existence (as it had been), to the meditativeness of the ground itself! It was connected with the centre of its very self, and then the world, the world, the world, began to rush about it, the world after which it had named itself. For the Ground truly was the world. Except that it had had time to think until now, it had managed — it had managed to contemplate. But now, so much was happening; motion was simply marching and marching over it, as if it wanted to destroy the ground's stability, the steadfastness of its own pedestal. So much was happening! Animals, people, trees, plants, houses and birdhouses, and soon chairs and chairs, and windows and roofs, and doves in Venice, and then skyscrapers, yes, the Ground wondered: "Now everything on me is different, but I'm still known by one name.

I'm still 'the Ground', as if nothing has happened." The Ground comforted itself a bit with the steadfastness of its name, and won back some of its former stability. But that wasn't enough for the Ground, because something was constantly sprouting from it — bees, hives, and little teapots, and bracelets for thin wrists, and birds rising into the air, partly close to the Ground, its complementary pairs — all this made it confused and unsure. The Ground didn't understand anything on it, and yet it felt responsible for all those incomprehensible, unusual beings. It was the last step, there was nothing that could cut the ground out beneath its feet! Chills ran across its body, now thicker, at the very thought. It was the final degree, the last stair just before the bottom... At that moment, the Ground noticed all those different shapes, composed of the same things, wandering about it; all those outlines whose flatness reflected all other standing, brimful shapes. The Ground found external unity and harmony in the chaos of living and non-living information upon its surface. It had seen what united everything, which meant the Ground no longer had to bother with schizophrenic differences, and yet could still dream of its steadfast flatness undisturbed by various verticalities. The ground felt shadows, shadows of all different things tickling it, cleaning it like great brooms, or simply existing steadfast upon it beneath the Sun, just like fish exist in water! It had finally found a world that truly belonged to it. The Ground thought: "Shadows are also all different, and yet they are called by one name. They are all 'shadows.'"... The stone fell from its heart, or rather all the beating hearts of various creatures fell from a stone to the ground; the Ground found unity in the eclectic reality on it and around it. Instead of observing people and wars, hospital rooms and births, or perhaps cheetahs scratching at trees with their claws, it observed shadows in which birth was equated to murder, shadows in which the inanimate melted with the animate, and even when the entire world lay together "in one single shadow," the Ground didn't get involved. The shadows respected it, belonged to it entirely, merged with it completely except when the façade of a building falsely presented itself as the Ground for a moment... But this affair would be brief, and the shadow would belong to it once again. And however restless some of them might have been, roaming, as if they wanted to run away from the Ground forever to attain revelation somewhere in the dark of space, they could never leave. The Ground would always stop their flying bodies with its steadfastness. Somewhere in that pairing between the Ground and shadow, a balancing of time, motion, and stillness took place... All other things, living and meaty, pressed at the Ground with their weight, and it was the verticality of this very weight that always yearned to take them somewhere far from the Earth. But the limitedness of their own bodies always brought them back, chastened, until they finally broke apart in the Ground, losing their shadow forever. The shadows, however, were different. They ceaselessly appeared and disappeared, died and were born, and every day, when a body would cast a shadow again, it would be a new shadow, never the one from the day before. And so countless shadows died every day, regardless of whether the bodies that had cast them were alive or not. It didn't matter to the shadows. They were always new, playful, monotone fairies, birds constantly showing the Big Bang on the façades, the explosion of everything, the melding of everything, the creation of the world. Vanishing while staying. Staying while vanishing. Stay-vanish — that is what the shadows did. And everything else on Earth, all those different colours, were more inclined to depart, but then their own shadows would pull them back down to Earth, it seemed, to the flatness of the Ground. At that point, the Ground suddenly realised why the shadows clung so close to it, why they belonged to it so truly. Only the Ground itself had no shadow! The final degree, the last step! The camera continued sweeping along that straight line, and now everything was full of shadows, but nowhere was there a shadow of the Ground. The Ground thought: "All the shadows are upon me now, but I'm still known by the same name, although I have no shadow. Shouldn't my name, then, belong to the world of shadow, and not to the world of breath like other names?" Nothing had changed, and yet the Ground became unhappy once again. How to stay stable in such a situation? So lonely. From whatever perspective it looked at the world — the world that contained it, which was the world itself — the Ground was different from everything on it. For it was not ON, it simply was. At that moment, the Ground felt a sudden need to also become ON. It drew up all the energy from its depths — all those dead people, animals, and their shadows, never to exist again — and cracked a few humps into its flatness. This is how the first volcano ON earth came about, and the first mountain, which immediately cast a sharp, tall shadow on the ground, a shadow of the Ground's very own matter that, like all other shadows, resembled all other shadows. Finally, the Ground belonged to the world, but it didn't even suspect that it had just given up its own immortality. Had it remained nothing more than a flat line, a bare, polished trail, the final step with no shadow, the line never would have disappeared. This way, the Earth joined all other mortals ON it. The mountains and volcanoes nullified the last steps. Everything became dust.

A Bloodless Story

I got all my materials ready in advance, like a child about to do his homework.

What I was planning on altering was as compact as a Swiss army knife, but the real Swiss one had been replaced with an ordinary kitchen knife, the sharp fin of a shark.

As if I were intending to enjoy the comfort of my own home, I stretched my legs out on the table. My feet twitched from left to right in a quick rhythm. Buzzing, tireless flies.

The decision ripened into reality. I would put them to sleep!

As soft as if I were cutting a slice of bread, I sawed off my left foot, and then my right one.

I cut them as carefully as if I were trying not to cut them.

Having decided to switch to a sitting position, I moved my legs (now more akin to sticks) from the table. I put my palm on the table, fanning my fingers as if I were planning to paint my nails.

And chop!

Go on, pointer finger, you smart-ass — fly! What good are you to me? Most of the time I point you away from me anyway; I only use you to explain things.

After a job well done, my gaze rested on my thumb, a digit so ripe for the guillotine...

"Just one more..." I thought, as if I were treating myself to one last piece of chocolate.

In cold blood, I severed his taut head and wrinkled body, satisfied with the knowledge that texting was a thing of the past. So much for his endless optimism!

After having so elegantly dealt with the two, I decided to execute the rest as well.

"All or nothing," I thought. "Fingers crossed!" I mumbled, ironically.

Chop — the middle finger joined the feast of digits. Cigarettes were now ancient history.

This particular finger had found himself in the middle, and so he'd never had the chance to be independent, to develop his own personality. Trapped on all sides, he had felt a constant pressure. Truly the monkey in the middle, and no middle ground in sight…!

Then, I came to the ring finger.

What to do with him? His only goal in life was to wear a mark, anyways. Chop — this was the kinder way for him to lose his head.

Having reached the final, "pinky finger," I took a moment to observe him cautiously. I liked him, the cute little thing! I had never had any particularly great need for him, and that's why he was especially dear to me.

For art's sake, I let him live! Now I can finally take a little break.

Nearly all of my limbs are as calm as teeth, those immobile bones that sit quietly in our mouths our entire lives, never cracking like the other calcified creations. Maybe that's why they're so high-strung! It isn't easy to stay calm as you wait to just fall out one day — plop! — like a pebble into the water. Teeth, solid objects within man that fall outside the perceptible.

The idea annoys me — it really gets my dander up! Who cares about hair, nails, eyelashes? It's all worthless.

I stand up from the table on my peg-legs and head to the bathroom.

I'm really not in the mood to wait for my teeth to start falling out some day. I'm impatient. Best get it over with straight away!

I begin plucking out my teeth like blades of grass. It's unbelievable how easily they go...

My mouth begins to turn into a harmless, soft hole, like a vagina. More and more of the murderous spikes pile up on the shelf. Food becomes a thing of the past, except I can still lick ice cream. I can also still kiss, because I've decided to spare my tongue. It's inseparable from both meat and words. It clings to my interior like a little black dress to Marilyn Monroe's figure.

I walk back to the table on my own two sticks.

What to do with the hand that so faithfully followed me on my mission?

I observe it regretfully. I'd rather keep it, because it was finally kind to me... But I can't. A deal is a deal. All or nothing!

At any rate, that hand often does things it doesn't feel like doing.

I won't stand for it.

I observe the candle, which I had calculatedly left burning on the table.

I move my extended, female fingers over to it, and the fire begins licking at them.

It swallows my life line and heart line, but I'm still here.

My nails slowly turn into burnt pieces of paper.

Soon, I plunge my stumps into a bowl of water. Because my wrist is the border up to which I have decided to become air. The room is filled with the scent of burning flesh, mixed with the scent of flowers from outside.

I put my legs on the table and intend to enjoy the comfort of my own home.

I feel like a tree whose hair is the only wild thing on it.

I still have eyes, ears, a nose, a vagina… Organs that let me receive without having to do anything. I simply open my eyes and the image is here. It gives itself to me, the window stretches out beneath me, and the sky through it.

I feed on the sounds from the park, and my ears don't have to run circles around the house or chew on notes.

These organs long only for dreams, and only when they become very, very heavy.

I've finally turned inward.

Wooden, I begin to flow.

The telephone, my additional, extended limb, rings in the distance. Let it ring — my life is finally in my hands!

Epilogue

THE INNER WORLD

In the first mouth — in Adam's boundless mouth — something happened that altered the further course of heavenly events. Let us imagine this, the stage on which everything unfolded, just as the world today unfolds in our own mouths...

The stage, a moist, steep cave, begins with soft, heart-shaped lips, and ends further on in a little opening that slips into the unknown. In the middle hangs the uvula — "booiiiinng!" Sometimes, most often when Adam speaks, the mouth is open, and it is closed when he thinks and dreams. Right after the entrance to the cave, a rampart of teeth juts from the upper and lower sides of the jaw... The rest is nothing more than meat lining all sides of the cave, and various characters that stroll about the red carpet of the tongue... Whilst Adam sleeps, they begin to express themselves...

"We are the border, the invincible rampart of this fortress...!" the teeth exclaimed, beginning their litany. "If there were wars in the Garden of Eden, we would be the first to launch ourselves into the abyss of the outside world in the name of the mouth! We would be the border where Thought would adorn the garments of the word, roaring: 'To battle!' But now, all it does is whisper 'I love you, I love you' into Eve's ear all day, as if there isn't anything else in Eden to whisper about... As if our keen spears have been predestined to do no more than chew tomatoes! Why, is eating truly our sole purpose?

"Oh, how we envy the fingers, Adam's accursed fingers, which we sometimes see through the mouth, watching them create. Unlike us, they fill in the emptiness, they create order through chaos! The fingers, our other half. How we would love to be fingers, to change places with them! Fingers in the mouth, and teeth on the hands!" In their white robes, the choir of incisors, molars, and canines carolled in consonance.

Just then, a joyous, naked being jumped onto the soft carpet of the tongue, its left half red and its white half black. The face of the being was shrouded in fog, as if a frosted glass had been pulled over it.

"Ho, ho, *teeth!* Waxing philosophical again, are we? While Adam sleeps, your individuality comes to the fore!" said the being as it slithered across the tips of all the teeth as if sliding down the edge of a single wall.
"Ah, Miss *Thoughtword* has awoken from her hibernation… So, tell us, why must you always provoke us? Is it not perhaps because of your bipolarity? Your dependence on all of us, the tongue and the teeth… Only while Adam sleeps can you truly realise yourself and be *Thoughtword*… While Adam is awake, you're either *Thought* or *Word*, and we are the machine that always converts you. The only thing you share in both of the aforementioned cases is the fact that you are invisible."
"Meeow…" the quivering being squealed, hiding behind a molar.
"What now? Identity issues, eh?" the teeth clamoured. "Then you should learn to keep your tongue firmly *behind* your teeth! You turn into such a windbag when you loosen up. When Adam wakes up, we'll get the tongue to throw you out, and you'll become a word for Eve. Or maybe you'd prefer to remain nothing more than a warm thought about her?"
"It's so stressful going in and out all the time, in and out! The constant transformations! *This* is my true self! Maybe it's

undefined and doesn't know what to do with itself, but that's who I am. I would give everything to just be left alone for a bit!" She began to stamp her feet. "I can't constantly think about other beings and things. I want to think about myself a bit... Eve? What does she have to do with me?!" The being began to cry, and the veil of fog she wore across her face began to fill with water, becoming a little lake dripping with tears.

"Oh, love..." the teeth roared again. "What do you think *we* have to do with Eve?! And we constantly have to nibble her neck or her earlobe! Like complete losers, so far from the hands! Sometimes, we get the urge to just muster all our strength and bite through her jugular with gusto! But at the last moment, we manage to collect ourselves and just keep nibbling, as if we were baby teeth... Here in this paradise, we're not allowed to create a real world, or to take a life. All forms of expression have been taken away from us. What kind of paradise is this?!" If they had had them, the teeth would have rolled their eyes. "Adam forgets that you and we are a rich, inner world. He shouldn't just instrumentalise us so cruelly..."

"Don't say such awful things! Your thoughts fly in the face of my thoughtwords and Adam's thoughts, words, and actions. If I had the power, I'd take away your ability to think!" shrieked *Thoughtword*. She hid in the gap between the two front teeth and continued crying.

"Each of us has our own nature, *Thoughtword*, and in an ideal paradise, it would have to be expressed... But it seems paradise is only possible if it's built by the spineless," the teeth stated in an unenergetic, conciliatory tone.

Thoughtword hesitated a bit before coming back out onto the soft carpet of the sleeping tongue.

"But murder? You can't do that in paradise!" she said with a hint of doubt, but then immediately changed the subject, trying to turn the tables in her own favour. "So, you'll be merciful and won't throw me out when Adam wakes up? I need a few days' rest… To really look into who the true me is," the being asked the thundering jury of teeth, her tone now honeyed and shrill, the tears now completely dry on her foggy face.

"*Thoughtword*, even though we're always bickering, we have more in common than we think. Maybe we even share the same goals," a molar answered in a baritone, speaking for the entire choir of teeth. "You don't know who you are because you don't have time to develop, someone or something always interrupts you… We teeth know who we are, but because this inner world has been put together all wrong, we're convinced we deserve much more than we get! Instead of worshiping us as holy idols balanced on a mysterious border between worlds, they use us to bite and chew! We, coated in enamel and brilliant in our importance, have been turned into ordinary workers!" With the help of the gums, the teeth puffed up to look larger and stronger.

Thoughtword recoiled in fear, rendered speechless for a moment.

"But, but, but, but, but, but," she stuttered. "I knnnnnnnnow how important you are, I knnnnnnnnnnnnnnnow that you're the mmmmmmmagical border of mmmmmmmy everyday painful transformation. Only I pass your spears unharmed and unchewed… Instead, your soft touches transform me into consonants, into T, D, S, L, C… You create me, a pronounced word — some other, external me…"

"Are you trying to comfort us now?" the teeth bellowed inexorably. "Don't you know you're impossible to catch, and thus worthless?!" they bellowed even more forcefully. "You collapse into dust the moment you transform. Soon after you move past us and the lips... You're eternally air, emptiness, nought. You simply aren't important... We couldn't even bite through your jugular if we wanted to..."

At these words, *Thoughtword* once again began to cry bitterly, and her little lake dried up. For just a moment, her face showed through — a tiny, wrinkled, thin rag — before she quickly wrapped it up again in its cloud of fog.

"Oh come now, *Thoughtword*, enough with the antics. This is already the fifth time you've started crying! You're not a little child... You've existed for quite some time now," the teeth said in a seemingly hopeless voice. "Instead of enjoying the fact that you're currently who you want to be, with a little body, a foggy head, and all your words and thoughts, you break down and fall into the abyss. Enough of that. Anyway, let's get down to business."

At these words, *Thoughtword* stood up as straight as a soldier and began to listen with interest.

"Bravo. You see, you can do it. Unusual beings require a firm hand! At any rate, since all of us here want to free ourselves of slavery and attain free will, the time has come to take action. We know who needs to be taken care of first! That witless tongue, that slimy hunting dog beneath your feet. He always does just what Adam tells him to! Now he's sleeping because Adam is sleeping, and when he wakes up, he'll wake up and kiss Eve! Like some stupid mollusc! I don't know how we've managed to put up with him... Oh, this eternal dungeon, full of characters that never go anywhere — instead, they just keep stuffing themselves with new crumbs," the teeth moaned desperately. "*Thoughtword*, we've come up with the entire plan. You just have to keep your lips sealed and do what we tell you to," the teeth continued more calmly. "We'll make sure you get yours, we promise. You won't get left with the short end of the stick."

"Fine, then I entrust myself to your teeth! Poor little me — what can I do on my own? I have no choice, I have to join the majority... Just, please, don't change the world! We mustn't ever change the world..." *Thoughtword* shrugged sadly in deference, scrawny and ragged on the rough red carpet of the sleeping tongue.

"Slow down, *Thoughtword*... Stop making requests or we'll turn you back into nothing more than (Adam's) thought! Now listen up. Our plan is simple. While Adam is sleeping, we'll slowly clamp down on the tongue, and there will be no way he can beat us! He's so important and yet powerless, just like the language he serves so faithfully... As soon as we clamp down on him, you'll have your chance to sneak out regardless of Adam's orders and be free. You won't stay inside — you'll escape to the outside, where you can finally be *Thoughtword!* See how well we take care of you? Hahahahaha!" The teeth sounded just the faintest bit malevolent, thought *Thoughtword*.

But she didn't say a word to their malevolence. Instead, she got ahead of herself and asked the teeth what they stood to gain from it.

"You'll see... Patience, patience. Now it's time to get to work," the teeth answered ceremoniously.

Thoughtword noticed how terrifyingly monumental the teeth were, as tall and serious as a mountain. How could anyone ever laugh at the mountains? Brrrr, a shiver ran through *Thoughtword's* tiny body — impressions seemed to be filling her more and more, and it seemed to her that she was becoming more and more autonomous.

℘

Suddenly, this situation vanished, just like all situations in the world can vanish suddenly. Both the teeth-individualists and *Thoughtword* were suddenly erased from the stage… Everything they had said and talked about vanished. No curtain fell as in a classical theatre — instead, Adam suddenly began to talk in his sleep and opened his mouth, and so his tongue awoke obediently as well. But, where was *Thoughtword* now, where were the teeth-individualists now? Did they even exist, seeing as she had been transformed into *Word*, while the teeth simply became a means by which to create the consonants T, D, S, L, C…

"LeT me go, LeT me go, STop CHasing afTer me! I won'T heSiTaTe To uSe forCe!" Adam spurted forth from his mouth into the outside world. His body began to flail, and he set upon Eve with his fists.

His blows woke her from her sleep, and she began to shake him worriedly.

"Hey, Adam, wake up! Were you having a nightmare? I didn't know they even existed in paradise… Come here, I'll take care of you," Eve sighed.

At that point, Adam suddenly screamed. He opened his eyes wide in shock, as if he wanted to outgrow himself through his eye sockets, to become nothing more than a lens and a pupil. Just to prove that reality was what he saw now, and everything he had dreamt an illusion.

As if he had been underwater for a long time and barely caught his breath, he hugged Eve both tightly and weakly at the same time.

"I'll be here as long as I live," Eve said, returning his embrace. "What did you dream?"

"That they were chasing me and I had nowhere left to run. I came to the edge of a cliff but couldn't make myself jump. I could only see their teeth and hands. I couldn't see their faces."

"Unusual."

"Yes."

"Nightmares seem like real problems in paradise. As if dreams are closer to reality here, because in reality, no one is after us. Which means that maybe someone really is after you."

"It's possible."

"Or maybe it's just your subconscious talking. Maybe it's nothing. Everything is fine so long as only our dreams are dark. There have to be dark dreams, even in paradise."

"Right," answered Adam absently.

"Come closer, snuggle up to me. Try and fall asleep."

Suddenly, this situation vanished, just like all situations in the world can vanish suddenly. Everything they had said and talked about faded away. Adam fell asleep, and his subservient tongue followed him on the same path. Where is Adam now? Where is Eve now?

☙

"*Thoughtword*?! Let's get right down to work! There's no more time. You see how unsafe everything is... Even though we always wake up amidst heavenly immortality, our mouths or eyes wide open. Are you ready?!" the teeth thundered.

"*Thoughtword*!?! Where are you? We can't hear you. You're not off somewhere crying again are you? Oh no… All the stress you're putting on us is going to make us cry in the end…!"

"Thought! Word?!" The teeth called cacophonously at all sides.

But *Thoughtword* thought that she didn't want to cry anymore. She ground her teeth and waited in silence for the teeth to throw her out like never before. She was a bit afraid of new experiences, but she didn't want to feel sorry for herself. She just relaxed her tiny little body and waited, invisible like a chameleon, on the tongue's body…

"*Thoughtword*, ready or not, we're going to bite down on the tongue!"

The teeth suddenly clamped down viciously on the tongue's slimy body and fixed it in place. *Thoughtword* slipped silently through the teeth, mixed together with the meat of the tongue, and she just barely found a tiny bubble of air for herself. Her invisible body trembled in fear — this was the point where she was used to becoming sound, melody. She would experience a powerful transformation, feel herself becoming only a wrinkled stream of air. Her adrenaline would rush, as if she were driving 500 kilometres per hour! This is why she would always be especially happy when her transformation began with the word "jet plane…!" But now her little body trembled with fear, because absolutely nothing was happening. *Thoughtword* felt the smooth, toothed passage through which she passed, and she touched the enamel of the teeth from the outside… Then her bare, invisible feet walked in a circle across the soft lips… Even though nothing happened, *Thoughtword's* tiny body was thrilled… A thrill she had never experienced before ran through her entire body.

Led by this feeling, she jumped from the warm lips onto a hard, wooden table. She looked around and saw Adam sitting, lost in thought and smoking. She saw his hand take a piece of coal and begin writing signs she didn't understand on the table, and for the first time, she saw herself as equal to Adam, just as the person she wanted to be — as *Thoughtword*. The signs he was drawing in coal on the wall and table might have been her branching body... The fingers only made marks — they weren't creating anything tangible, to the great satisfaction of the teeth...

He continued scribbling. Eva's voice no longer reached him... Completely absorbed in the inner world, Adam forgot to eat... The teeth simply existed. They didn't grind or cut anything. But, regardless, the skin on his body and fingers soon disappeared. The uvula, "boooiiiinng", evaporated along with the tongue. The moles fell from his face and his skull showed through.

The teeth spoke again. They sounded distant, no longer a part of his face, but of his skull. Their voices were nearly crystalline.

"We are the border, the invincible rampart of this fortress. We, the only bone that juts out from death into life and from life into death. White and bare." "Where is Adam now? Where is Eva now?" the voices of the teeth echoed out again.

Suddenly, this situation continued, just like all situations in the world can continue. The stage spread expansively in front of the rampart of teeth. Into the empty audience, into the dark side of an underground world... There, Cain soon beat his brother to death with his fingers, and they became nothing more than a tool, just like the teeth... *Thoughtword*, on the other hand, grabbed firmly onto paper, where she remains to this day. Her reddish-black body, in reddish-black worlds bordered with teeth… Simultaneously, the *written word* and mortality were born.